The critics on Jostein Gaarder's previous international
bestseller *SOPHIE'S WORLD*

'A marvellously rich book. Its success boils down to
something quite simple – Gaarder's gift for communicat-
ing ideas' *Guardian*

'An Alice in Wonderland for the 90s ... already *Sophie's
World* is being talked up as philosophy's answer to
Stephen Hawking's *A Brief History of Time* ... this is a sim-
ply wonderful, irresistible book' *Daily Telegraph*

'Remarkable ... what Jostein Gaarder has managed to do
is condense 3000 years of thought into 400 pages; to sim-
plify some extremely complicated arguments without
trivialising them ... *Sophie's World* is an extraordinary
achievement' *Sunday Times*

'Challenging, informative and packed with easily
grasped, and imitable, ways of thinking about difficult
ideas' *Independent on Sunday*

'*Sophie's World* is a whimsical and ingenious mystery
novel that also happens to be a history of philosophy ...
What is admirable in the novel is the utter unpreten-
tiousness of the philosophical lessons ... which manages
to deliver Western philosophy in accounts that are crys-
tal clear' *Washington Post*

'A terrifically entertaining and imaginative story wrapped
round its tough, thought-provoking philosophical heart'
Daily Mail

'Seductive and original ... *Sophie's World* is, as it dares to
congratulate itself, "a strange and wonderful book" ' *TLS*

Jostein Gaarder was born in Oslo in 1952. *Sophie's World*, the first of his books to be published in English, has been published in 40 languages and has been a bestseller in each of them.

By the same author

Sophie's World
The Solitaire Mystery

THE
CHRISTMAS
MYSTERY

Jostein Gaarder

TRANSLATED BY
Elizabeth Rokkan

ILLUSTRATED BY
Rosemary Wells

ORION

An Orion paperback
First published in Great Britain by Phoenix House in 1996
This paperback edition published in 1997 by Orion Books Ltd,
Orion House, 5 Upper St Martin's Lane, London WC2H 9EA

Originally published in Norwegian under the title *Julemysteriet*,
copyright © 1992 by H. Aschehoug & Co
(W. Nygaard), Oslo

A CIP catalogue record for this book is available
from the British Library.

ISBN: 0 75380 168 X

Printed and bound in Great Britain by
Clays Ltd, St Ives plc

CONTENTS

the
FIRST
OF DECEMBER

... perhaps the clock hands had become so tired of going in the same direction year after year that they had suddenly begun to go the opposite way instead ...

DUSK WAS FALLING. The lights were on in the Christmas streets, thick snowflakes were dancing between the lamps. The streets were crowded with people.

Among all these busy persons were Papa and Joachim, who had gone into town to buy an Advent calendar. It was their last chance, because tomorrow would be the first of December. They were sold out at the newsstand and in the big bookstore at the market.

Joachim tugged his father's hand hard and pointed at a tiny shop window where a brightly coloured Advent calendar was leaning against a pile of books.

'There!' he said.

Papa turned back. 'Saved!'

They went into a little bookshop that Joachim thought looked old and worn out. Books stood tightly packed on shelves along all the walls from floor to ceiling, all of them different. A large pile of Advent calendars lay on the counter. There were two kinds, one with a picture of Santa Claus with a sled and reindeer and the other with a picture of a barn with a tiny little elf eating porridge out of a big bowl.

Papa held up the two calendars.

'There are plastic figures in this one and chocolate ones in that,' he said, 'but the dentist won't be too happy about that.'

Joachim examined the two calendars. He didn't know which one he wanted.

'It was different when I was a boy,' continued Papa.

'How do you mean?'

'Then there was only a tiny picture behind each door, one for each day. But it was exciting every morning, trying to guess what the picture would be. Then we opened it . . . well, we *opened* it, you see. It was like opening the door to a different world.'

Joachim had noticed something. He pointed to one of the walls of books. 'There's an Advent calendar over there too.'

He ran over to fetch it and held it up to show Papa. It had a picture of Joseph and Mary bending over the baby Jesus in the manger. The Three Wise Men from the East were kneeling in the background. Outside the stable were the shepherds with their sheep, and angels floating down from the sky. One of them was blowing a trumpet.

The colours of the calendar were faded as if it had been lying in the sun all summer, but the picture was so beautiful that Joachim almost felt sorry for it.

'I want this one,' he said.

Papa smiled. 'You know, I don't think this one's for sale. I think it must be very old. Maybe as old as I am.'

Joachim wouldn't give up. 'None of the doors are open.'

'But it's only here on display.'

'I want it,' repeated Joachim. 'I only want one that's like none of the others.'

The bookseller came up – a man with white hair. He looked surprised when he saw the Advent calendar.

'Beautiful!' he exclaimed. 'And genuine – yes, original. It almost looks home-made.'

'He wants to buy it,' explained Papa, pointing at Joachim. 'I'm trying to explain that it's not for sale.'

The man raised his eyebrows.

'Did you find it here? I haven't seen one like that for years.'

'It was in front of all the books,' said Joachim.

'Oh, it must be old John up to his tricks again,' said the bookseller.

Papa stared at the man. 'John?'

'Yes, he's a strange character. He sells roses in the market, but where he gets them from, nobody knows. Sometimes he comes in and asks for a glass of water. In summer when it's hot he'll pour the last drops over his head before he goes out again. He's poured a few drops over me a couple of times, too. To thank me for the water he sometimes leaves one or two roses on the counter; or he'll put an old book on the bookshelf. Once he put a photograph of a young woman in the window. It was from a country far away – maybe that's where he comes from himself. "Elisabet", it said on the photo.'

'And now he's left an Advent calendar?'

'Yes, evidently.'

'There's something written on it,' said Joachim. He read aloud: 'MAGIC ADVENT CALENDAR. Price 75 øre.'

The bookseller nodded. 'In that case it must be very old.'

'May I buy it for 75 øre?' asked Joachim.

The man laughed. 'I think you should have it for nothing. You'll see, old John had you in mind.'

'Thank you, thank you, thank you,' replied Joachim, on his way out of the bookshop already.

Papa shook the bookseller's hand and followed Joachim out on to the pavement.

Joachim hugged the calendar tight. 'I'll open it tomorrow,' he said.

Joachim kept waking up that night, thinking about the bookseller and John with his roses. Once he went to the bathroom and drank water from the tap, and thought of John pouring water over his head.

Most of all he thought about the magic Advent calendar. It was as old as Papa, but all the same, nobody had opened any of the doors. Before he went to bed he had found all the doors from 1 to 24. The twenty-fourth was of course Christmas Eve, and that door was four times bigger than the others, covering almost the whole of the manger in the stable.

Where had the magic Advent calendar been for over forty years? And what would happen when he opened the first door?

When he woke up again and it was seven o'clock, he reached up for the calendar, which was hanging above his bed, to open the first door. His fingers were so impatient and nervous that it was difficult to get hold of it properly. At last he managed to loosen a tiny corner, and the door opened slowly.

Joachim gazed in to a picture of a toyshop. Among all the toys and the people were a little lamb and a small girl, but he couldn't look at the picture in detail, for just as he opened the door something fell out on to his bed. He bent down and picked it up.

It was a thin sheet of paper, folded over and over. When he had smoothed it out he saw that there was writing on both sides. So he read what was on the paper.

THE LAMBKIN

'ELISABET!' HER MOTHER called after her. 'Come back, Elisabet!'

Elisabet Hansen had been standing staring at the big pile of teddy bears and furry animals while her mother was buying Christmas presents for the cousins who lived at Toten. All of a sudden a little lamb shot out of the pile. It jumped on to the floor and looked around. It had a bell round its neck, and the bell started to jingle in competition with all the cash registers.

How could a toy suddenly come to life? Elisabet was so surprised that she started to chase the lamb. It was running across the wide floor of the department store in the direction of the moving staircase.

'Lambkin, lambkin!' she called after it.

The lamb was already on the staircase, which was moving down to the floor below. The stairs moved quite quickly, and the lamb sprang even quicker, so that Elisabet had to run faster than the stairs and the lamb together if she was going to catch up with it.

'Come back, Elisabet!' repeated her mother severely.

But Elisabet had already jumped on to the staircase. She could see the lamb running through the ground floor where they sold underwear and ties.

As soon as she had solid ground beneath her feet again, she went the same way as the lamb. It had managed to bound out on to the street where the snowflakes were dancing among the chains of Christmas lights hanging above the street. Elisabet knocked over a stand of winter gloves and followed it.

Out in the noisy street she could barely hear the bell

jingling. But Elisabet did not give up. She was determined to stroke the lamb's soft fleece.

'Lambkin, lambkin!'

The lamb sprang across the road against a red light. Perhaps it thought a red man meant 'Go!' and a green man meant 'Stop!'. Elisabet thought she had heard that all sheep were colour blind. At any rate, the lamb didn't stop, so Elisabet couldn't stop either. She was going to catch up with the lamb even if she had to follow it to the ends of the earth.

The cars tooted their horns, and a motorbike had to swerve on to the pavement to avoid colliding with Elisabet or the lamb. The people doing their Christmas shopping all stared. They didn't often see a little girl running across the road after a lamb. In any case, it was strange to be running after a lamb in the middle of winter.

As they ran, Elisabet heard the church clock striking three. She noticed it specially, because she knew she had come to town on the five o'clock bus. Perhaps the hands had become so tired of going in the same direction year after year that they had suddenly begun to go the opposite way instead. Elisabet thought that clocks, too, might get bored with doing the same thing all the time.

But there was something else as well. When Elisabet had gone into the department store, it had been almost completely dark. Now it was suddenly light again, and that was curious, because there had been no night in between.

As soon as the lamb had a chance, it found a road leading out of town, and trotted on towards a small wood. It sprang on to a path between tall pine trees. Now the lamb had to slow down a little, for the path was covered with all the snow that had been falling during the past few days.

Elisabet went after it. It was difficult for her to run now, too. But the lamb had four legs which were dragging in the snow, while she had only two. Perhaps that would help her to gain on it.

Her mother's cries had been drowned long ago by the noise in the street. Soon she couldn't even hear street sounds. But something was still singing in her ears: 'Shall we buy this one, or both of them? What do you think, Elisabet?'

Perhaps the reason the lamb had come to life and run away from the big store was that it could no longer bear to listen to the cash registers and the talk about buying and selling. And perhaps that was why Elisabet was following it. She had never enjoyed shopping.

JOACHIM LOOKED UP FROM the sheet of paper that had fallen out of the magic Advent calendar. What he had read was so amazing.

He had always liked secrets. Now he remembered the little box with the key in it, the one Grandma had bought him in Poland. Mama and Papa had made him a solemn promise that they would never look for the key and open the box when Joachim was asleep or at school. It would have been as bad as opening someone else's letters, they had said.

Up to now Joachim hadn't had any real secrets to hide in the box, but now he put the paper from the Advent calendar there, turned the key, and hid it under his pillow. So when Mama and Papa woke up and came to look at the Advent calendar too, they only saw the picture of the lamb in the department store.

'Do you remember?' asked Mama, looking up at Papa. 'It was just like that when we were small.'

Papa nodded. 'Then we could use our imagination on the little picture and make up the rest ourselves. It was much better than those plastic figures that end up being swallowed by a vacuum cleaner.'

Something was laughing inside Joachim. Only *he* knew that there had been a mysterious piece of paper inside the calendar.

He pointed at the picture of the lamb.

'The lamb has decided to run away from the shop,' he said, 'because it can't bear listening to the cash registers and the talk of buying and selling. But there's a little girl called Elisabet in the shop, and she's begun running after the lamb because she wants to stroke it.'

'Isn't that just what I said?' said Papa. 'What does the boy want with plastic figures?'

For the rest of the day Joachim wondered whether Elisabet would catch up with the lamb so that she could stroke its fleece. Would he find out tomorrow?

For then there'd surely be another little piece of paper?

the
SECOND
OF DECEMBER

... I know of a short cut,

and that's the path we're taking now ...

JOACHIM WOKE UP BEFORE Mama and Papa the next morning too, but then he nearly always did. He sat up and looked at the Advent calendar. Only now did he notice a little lamb lying at the feet of one of the shepherds. Wasn't that strange? He had spent a long time looking at the picture with all the angels and the Wise Men, the shepherds and their sheep, but he had never noticed the lamb.

Perhaps it was because he had read about the lamb on the piece of paper that had fallen out of the calendar. But *that* lamb had jumped out of a modern shop – and the lamb on the Advent calendar had lived in Bethlehem, long ago. There were no cars and traffic lights then, and no big stores with escalators and cash registers. Besides, Elisabet had heard the church clock striking three, and surely there were no church clocks two thousand years ago? Joachim knew that that was when the baby Jesus was born.

Now he found the door with a number 2 on it, and opened it carefully. A folded piece of paper fell out of the calendar as the door slowly opened. He peeped in at a picture of a wood, where an angel stood with his arm round a little girl.

Joachim bent down and picked up the scrap of paper

that had fallen into the bed. He unfolded it and saw that something was written on it in tiny letters on both sides of the page. And he began to read.

EPHIRIEL

ELISABET HANSEN DIDN'T know how far nor how long she had run after the lamb, but when she set off through the town it had been snowing heavily. Now it had not only stopped snowing, there was no snow on the path either. Among the trees she could see blue anemones, coltsfoot and windflowers, and that was unusual, because it was very nearly Christmas.

She picked an anemone and looked at the blue petals carefully. Picking flowers at this time of year was every bit as mysterious as throwing snowballs at Midsummer.

It occurred to Elisabet that perhaps she had run so far that she had reached a country where it was summer all the year round. If not, she must have run for so long that spring and the warm weather had arrived already. In that case, she might still be in Norway, but then, what would have happened to Christmas?

While she stood wondering she heard the tinkle of a bell in the distance. Elisabet started running again and soon caught sight of the lamb. It had found a small grassy bank and was grazing on it greedily. The little creature had probably been very hungry. It had not had any grass to eat as long as it was winter. It had certainly not had a morsel of food as long as it had been a toy either, and that may have been for a very long time.

Elisabet crept up towards the lamb, but just as she was about to pounce on it in order to stroke it, it sprang away again.

'Lambkin, lambkin!'

Elisabet tried to keep up with it, but she tripped over a pine root and fell flat on the ground.

The worst of it was that she realised she was unlikely ever to catch up with the lamb. She had decided to follow it to the ends of the earth, but the earth was round, after all, so they might go on running round the world for ever, or at any rate until she grew up, and by then she might have lost interest in such things as lambs.

When she looked up she caught sight of a shining figure between the trees. Elisabet looked, wide-eyed, for it was neither an animal nor a human being. A pair of wings were sticking out of a robe as white as the lamb.

Elisabet had only just managed to get to know the world. She had learned what all the commonest animals were called, but she didn't know the difference between a tomtit and a yellowhammer. Nor between a camel and a dromedary, come to think of it. All the same, there was no mistaking what she was looking at now. Elisabet realised at once that the shining figure must be an angel. She had seen angels in books and pictures, but it was the first time she had seen one in real life.

'Fear not!' said the angel in a gentle voice.

Elisabet raised herself halfway up.

'You needn't think I'm afraid of you,' she replied, a little sulkily because she had fallen and hurt herself.

The angel came closer. It looked as if he was hovering just above the ground. It reminded Elisabet of her cousin Anna who could dance on the tips of her toes. The angel knelt down and stroked her gently on the nape of her neck with the tip of one of his wings.

'I said, "Fear not", to be on the safe side,' he said. 'We don't appear to humans very often, so it's best to be careful when we do. Usually people are frightened when they're visited by an angel.'

Suddenly Elisabet began to cry, not because she was afraid of angels, and not because she had hurt herself either. She didn't understand why she was crying until she heard herself sob, 'I wanted . . . to stroke the lamb.'

The angel nodded gracefully. 'I'm sure God wouldn't have created the lambs with such soft fleece unless He hoped someone would want to stroke it.'

'The lamb runs much faster than I do,' sobbed Elisabet, again, 'and it has twice as many legs too. Isn't that unfair? I can't see why a little lambkin should be in such a hurry.'

The angel helped her to her feet and said confidentially, 'It's going to Bethlehem.'

Elisabet had stopped crying. 'To Bethlehem?'

'Yes. To Bethlehem, to Bethlehem! For that's where Jesus was born.'

Elisabet was very surprised at what the angel said. In an attempt to hide her astonishment she began to brush soil and grass off her trousers. There were some nasty stains on her red jacket too.

'Then I want to go to Bethlehem,' she said.

The angel was dancing on the tips of his toes again on the path.

'That suits me,' he said, hovering above the ground. 'I'm going there too. So we might just as well keep each other company, all three of us.'

Elisabet had learned that she should never go anywhere

with people she didn't know. That certainly applied to angels as well. So she looked up at the angel and asked, 'What's your name?'

Elisabet had thought the angel was a man, but she wasn't quite sure. Now he curtseyed like a ballet dancer and said, 'My name is Ephiriel.'

'That sounds like a butterfly. Did you really say Ephiriel?'

'Just Ephiriel, yes. Angels have no mother or father, so we have no family name either.'

Elisabet sniffed for the last time. Then she said, 'I don't think we have time to talk any more if we're going all the way to Bethlehem. Isn't it a long way?'

'Yes indeed, it's very far – and a very long time ago. But I know of a short cut, and that's the path we're taking now.'

And with that they began to run. First the lamb, then Elisabet. The angel Ephiriel danced behind them.

As they ran, Elisabet felt sorry she hadn't asked the angel why it had suddenly become summer. But when she caught a glimpse of the lamb on the path in front of her, she didn't dare stop.

'Lambkin, lambkin!'

JOACHIM HURRIED TO hide the piece of paper in the secret box for which only he had the key.

It was John the flower-seller who had left the old calendar with the bookseller. Did he know about the scraps of paper too? Or was Joachim the only person in the whole world who knew the secret? After all, he was the only person who had opened the calendar.

But another thought struck him. Elisabet! he thought. Wasn't Elisabet the name of the lady whose picture John had put in the shop window?

Yes, it was, he was quite certain. Could it be the same Elisabet he was reading about in the magic Advent calendar? She was only a child, it's true, but the calendar was so old that she must have had plenty of time to grow up during all the years that had passed since then.

Mama and Papa came in that day too, to see the picture in the calendar.

'An angel,' whispered Mama solemnly.

'He's comforting Elisabet,' explained Joachim. 'You see, she was running so fast after the lamb that she fell and hurt herself.'

Mama and Papa smiled at each other. They probably thought Joachim was good at inventing stories. They didn't know that he wasn't inventing anything at all.

That day he had to get to school early, so there was no time for more talk about the Advent calendar. But Joachim thought about nothing else on his way to school.

So much snow had fallen during the past few days that it was heavy going across the big sports field. He thought how Elisabet had been floundering in snow when she had begun running after the lamb, but then it was suddenly summer. Surely that was impossible?

When he came home from school he had to let himself in. He got home a bit earlier than Mama nearly every day.

Joachim rushed to his room and looked up at the magic Advent calendar. It was still hanging there all right. During the day he had wondered whether it had only been a dream, for Joachim was always dreaming about the strangest things.

Now he was longing to know what the picture under the

number 3 was. Should he open the third door now? All he had to do was stick it back again afterwards and pretend he hadn't done it.

But that would be cheating. To cheat over Christmas would be even worse than cheating at cards. It was like peeping into parcels that were not to be opened until Christmas Eve. It was almost like stealing from yourself.

Mama soon came home from work and started to peel potatoes and carrots. Then Papa arrived, complaining that he had lost his driving licence.

'I can't understand it,' he said. 'Not in the car, not at the office, and not in my coat pocket either.'

'You're a real muddlehead,' said Joachim. Papa always said that to him when he couldn't find his pencil case or tidied his toys away.

That evening must have been the first time in his whole life that Joachim asked to go to bed early.

'You don't feel ill, do you darling?' asked Mama.

'No, of course not. But I'm looking forward so much to opening the magic Advent calendar that I can't wait.'

the
THIRD
OF DECEMBER

... like running before the wind – or like

rushing down a moving staircase ...

JOACHIM WOKE UP EARLY on the morning of the third of December. The Donald Duck clock that hung above his desk said a quarter to seven, so there was still half an hour to go until Mama and Papa's usual waking time.

He remembered that he'd dreamt about something strange, but he was not quite sure what. It had been something to do with the angel Ephiriel and the lamb.

He pulled himself up in bed and peered up at the magic Advent calendar. At the top of the picture several angels were floating down through the clouds in the sky. One of them was blowing a trumpet. That was to wake up all the sheep and the shepherds, of course.

Joachim imagined that the angel on the right of the picture must be Ephiriel. He was just as Joachim had thought Ephiriel might look, and he was smiling at Joachim, raising an arm as if he was trying to wave to him. The angel seemed clearer than yesterday.

Joachim got to his feet on the bed and opened the door with the number 3 on it. He saw a tiny little picture of a vintage car. He had seen that kind of old car once when he went to the Technical Museum with Grandpa.

Joachim didn't understand what a vintage car could have to do with Christmas, but then he picked up the little piece of paper that had fallen out of the calendar and down on to

his pillow. He snuggled down under the duvet and read what
was written on the sheet.

THE SECOND SHEEP

ELISABET AND THE ANGEL Ephiriel ran on after the lamb.
Soon they had left the wood behind and were going
down a narrow country lane. In the distance thick
smoke was rising from some tall factory chimneys.

'There's a town,' said Elisabet.

'That's Halden,' explained the angel. 'We're quite close to
Sweden.'

Suddenly they heard a clatter right behind them. Elisabet
turned and saw an old car driving towards them. Driving
the car was a man with a hat and coat and a black beard
who looked a bit like the picture of Great-grandpa on the
mantelpiece at home. As he passed, the man sounded the
horn and doffed his hat.

'That car must be terribly old!' exclaimed Elisabet.

'On the contrary, I think it was probably brand new,' said
Ephiriel.

'I always thought angels were much cleverer than humans.
But you don't seem to know much about cars,' said Elisabet,
sighing in frustration. But she didn't want to argue with the
angel, so she went on, 'But I suppose you don't drive cars in
heaven. I expect God has forbidden any kind of pollution.'

Ephiriel tried to hide a laugh. He pointed to a pile of
logs.

'Sit down here,' he said. 'You deserve a short rest, and
there's something important I have to tell you about our
journey to Bethlehem.'

Elisabet sat down and looked at the angel.

'Don't you get tired too?' she asked.

The angel shook his head. 'No, angels don't get tired. We're not made of flesh and blood. It's flesh and blood that get tired.'

Elisabet felt a bit embarrassed. Of course angels didn't get tired! If they did, they wouldn't have the strength to fly up and down between heaven and earth.

'Now can you tell me exactly where we are going, my dear?' asked the angel.

'To Bethlehem,' replied Elisabet.

'And what are we going to do there?'

'We're going to stroke the lamb, I suppose.'

The angel nodded. 'And we'll also welcome the baby Jesus into the world. He was called God's lamb, because He was just as kind and innocent as the little lamb's fleece is soft. We have to travel two thousand years backwards in time to the moment when Jesus was born.'

Elisabet put her hand to her mouth. 'But isn't it impossible to travel backwards in time?' she asked.

'Not at all,' said Ephiriel. 'Nothing is impossible for God, and I am here as God's messenger. We have a small part of the journey behind us already. Down there you see Halden, and we have arrived back at the beginning of the twentieth century. Do you understand?'

'I think so,' said Elisabet. 'And that means the car wasn't old after all.'

'No. It may have been brand new. I'm sure you noticed how proud the driver was when he sounded his horn. Not very many people owned cars then.'

Elisabet simply sat and stared, and Ephiriel continued.

'Since you began running after the lamb, more than fifty

years have gone by. We are running to Bethlehem through
time, going downhill through history on a diagonal line. It's
like running before the wind, or rushing down a moving
staircase.'

Elisabet nodded. She wasn't sure she understood everything the angel was saying, but she knew how clever it all
was.

'How do you know we're at the beginning of the twentieth
century?'

The angel raised his arm and pointed at a gold watch on
his wrist, decorated with a row of shining pearls. On its face
it said 1916.

'It's an angel watch,' he explained. 'It isn't quite as accurate
as other watches, but in heaven we're not too particular
about all the hours and minutes.'

'Why not?'

'We have the whole of eternity to see to,' replied the angel.
'And anyway, we never have to catch a bus to get to work
on time.'

Now Elisabet understood why the church clock had only
struck three even though it had been six or seven o'clock
when she ran from the shop, and why the snow had disappeared and it had suddenly become summer. She had run
backwards in time.

'You began running along the diagonal path as soon as
you started chasing the lamb,' continued the angel Ephiriel.
'That's when the long journey through time and space
began.'

Another car approached them from the opposite direction,
leaving a cloud of dust and sand behind that made Elisabet
cough. When the dust cloud had settled, she pointed up at
the road.

'There's our lamb again. But look – now there's a grown sheep as well!'

The angel nodded.

'Verily I say unto you, that sheep is going to Bethlehem too.'

With that they began to run. When Elisabet and Ephiriel had caught up with the lamb and the sheep, both of them bounded on as well.

'Lambkin, lambkin!' coaxed Elisabet.

But the lamb and the sheep would not be coaxed into standing still. They were going to Bethlehem, to Bethlehem!

They passed the outskirts of Halden and paused for a moment to look down at all the people walking in the streets and the market. The ladies were wearing long, colourful cotton dresses and large hats in different colours. Several cars were sputtering along the streets, but there were horses and carriages as well.

They left it behind them and soon came to a frontier station. A large signboard announced: 'Frontier. SWEDEN.'

Elisabet was brought up short.

'Do you think we'll be allowed to go into Sweden?'

The angel fluttered around her like an overgrown butterfly.

'They won't dare to stop a pilgrimage,' he replied. 'Besides, it's only a few weeks since Norway had the same king as Sweden.'

'May I look at your angel watch again?'

Ephiriel stretched out his arm. The watch said 1905.

Then they sped past two frontier guards, the lamb and the sheep first, and Elisabet and the angel Ephiriel just behind them.

'Halt!' shouted the frontier guards. 'In the name of the law!'

But they were already far into Sweden. And they had come a few years closer to the birth of Jesus.

JOACHIM SAT UP IN bed. So that was why there was a picture of an old car in the Advent calendar! That was why it had suddenly become summer, too.

Joachim made haste to lock the piece of paper with the story about Elisabet and Ephiriel into the secret box, in case Mama and Papa came into the bedroom. Afterwards he sat for a long time, thinking over what he had read.

Joachim was old enough to know that you can't really run backwards in time, but at least you can do it in your thoughts.

At school he had heard that a thousand years to mankind can seem like one single day to God. And the angel Ephiriel had told Elisabet that nothing is impossible for God.

Could Elisabet and the angel really have run backwards in time?

Soon he heard Mama on the landing. She opened the door to his room and asked, 'Have you opened the Advent calendar?'

He nodded, and Mama leaned over the calendar.

'A vintage car!' she exclaimed.

She sounded a bit surprised, almost disappointed. Perhaps she thought there ought to be pictures of angels and Christmassy things every day.

'It's because Elisabet and the angel Ephiriel have run to Sweden at the time when cars like that were brand new,' said Joachim. 'They're going to run all the way to Bethlehem.'

'I think you're a real little storyteller,' replied Mama, patting him on the head. She went into the bathroom.

Joachim felt a tickle in his tummy when he thought of all the clever things he knew, that Mama and Papa believed he was just making up. He decided on something even more clever. On Christmas Eve he'd put together all the pieces of paper that had come from the magic calendar and place the packet under the Christmas tree. Then he would write: 'To the best Mama and Papa in the world' on the outside of the packet.

It was rather a pity he had had this idea, because it made him look forward to Christmas even more, and though it was fun to have something to look forward to it was boring having to wait so long. When Joachim looked forward to something exciting, it almost gave him a headache.

That afternoon Papa complained that he still hadn't found his driving licence. In that case, he wasn't really allowed to drive, said Mama. But when Papa heard that, he snorted like a steam engine.

the
FOURTH
OF DECEMBER

... he scarcely had time to look surprised ...

WHEN JOACHIM WOKE up on Friday, the fourth of December, he made sure it was completely quiet in the house before he opened the fourth door in the calendar.

The picture showed a man in a light blue robe that looked a bit like a nightgown. In his hand he held a tall staff. But Joachim had no time to look at the picture properly, because a scrap of paper fell down into his bed. He unfolded it and read.

JOSHUA

ELISABET AND THE angel Ephiriel hurried after the sheep and the lamb. They passed a red log cabin and a few patches of crops in a clearing in the woods. From a rise Ephiriel pointed down at a lake.

'That's the biggest lake in Scandinavia,' he said. 'The watch shows that 1891 years have passed since Jesus was born, but we've only just arrived in Sweden.'

A strongly-flowing river ran out of the lake. A bridge arched over the river, and they walked over it to the other side.

'This is the River Göta,' said Ephiriel. 'We'll follow an old cart track along the river bank.'

'Lambkin, lambkin!' coaxed Elisabet, but the sheep and the lamb had already begun running again.

They passed a village, and saw people streaming along the road towards a red-painted church. Most of them were on foot, but some of them were sitting in big, horse-drawn carts. The men were dressed in black suits and black hats, and many of the women were in black as well. Some of them were carrying hymn books.

'It must be Sunday,' said Elisabet.

They paused for a moment and looked down at all the people. Suddenly a little boy noticed them, but he scarcely had time to look surprised, because at that same moment the angel Ephiriel began running again. Elisabet had to hurry to keep up. Once she turned and looked back, but all the people in front of the church had vanished. The horses and carts had vanished too.

When they had left the village behind, Elisabet turned to the angel and said, 'A little boy saw us, but nobody else noticed.'

'Splendid. We try not to attract too much attention. Sometimes we can't help someone catching sight of us, but a glimpse is quite enough.'

They ran on through woods and fields. Now and again they saw some people haymaking or reaping corn with scythes. Sometimes they had to take a roundabout way so as not to scare them.

Before long the sheep and the lamb found pasture that was so green and tempting that it dazzled the eyes.

'Now's our chance,' whispered Elisabet, 'if we go up to them carefully.'

But just then a man came walking towards them, wearing a blue tunic and holding a tall staff curved at the top. He said solemnly, 'Peace be with you who walk on the narrow way along the Göta River. My name is Joshua the shepherd.'

'Then you are one of us,' said Ephiriel.

Elisabet didn't understand what the angel meant by that,

but then the shepherd said, 'I am coming with you to the Holy Land, for I must be in the fields when the angels announce the glad tidings of the birth of Jesus.'

Then Elisabet had a bright idea.

'If you are a proper shepherd, perhaps you can herd the lamb in this direction.'

The shepherd bowed low. 'That's not difficult for a good shepherd.'

He went over to the sheep and the lamb, and the next moment the lamb was kneeling at Elisabet's feet. She knelt down and stroked its soft fleece.

'I think you must be the fastest furry animal in the world,' she said, 'but I caught you at last!'

The shepherd thumped his crook on the ground and said, 'To Bethlehem, to Bethlehem!'

The lamb and the sheep bounded away, the shepherd, the angel and Elisabet after them.

As they ran, they looked down on a cluster of red timber houses that Ephiriel explained was a town called Kungälv.

'That means "Kings Rock" and the town was given that name because the Scandinavian kings used to meet here to take counsel together. One of them was Sigurd Jorsalfar,' said the angel. '"Jorsalfar" means the pilgrimage to Jerusalem, and Sigurd was given that name because he had been on a pilgrimage to the Holy Land where Jesus was born.'

Then they ran past a city at the mouth of the Göta River, where women in long dresses and men wearing hats and carrying walking sticks were parading up and down the streets, sitting in fine coaches drawn by two horses.

'That's Gothenburg,' said Ephiriel. 'The time is 1814, and Denmark has had to hand over Norway to Sweden. Now Norway will get her own Constitution.'

Joshua the shepherd turned and waved to them.

'To Bethlehem!' he called. 'To Bethlehem!'

They sped on through Sweden.

J OACHIM HAD ONLY just managed to hide the paper from the Advent calendar in his secret box when his mother came into his room.

'And what was the picture today?' she asked.

Joachim knew he had no need to answer. Mama always wanted to look for herself.

She clasped her hands together.

'It must be one of the shepherds in the fields.'

'Why do you say "in the fields"?' asked Joachim.

Mama told him that there were often pictures of shepherds in the lovely old Advent calendars, because the angels had come to the shepherds in the fields to tell them that the baby Jesus had been born.

'They've come as far as Gothenburg,' explained Joachim.

'Gothenburg? Who are "they"?'

'Elisabet Hansen, the angel Ephiriel and Joshua the shepherd. They're going to Bethlehem, to Bethlehem!'

Mama stared at him in surprise. 'You mustn't let this old calendar get to you. They're only pictures.'

Joachim realised he couldn't go on telling Mama and Papa all he knew about Elisabet. If he did, he would never to able to keep the secret of the scraps of paper that he was going to give to Mama and Papa as a Christmas present.

He realised something else, too. He would have to try to talk to John. He was the only person who knew where the magic Advent calendar had come from. Perhaps he knew more about Elisabet Hansen. But how could Joachim meet John? He wasn't allowed to go to town and to the market by himself.

He had just come into the house from school that afternoon when someone rang the doorbell. It couldn't be Mama, because Joachim never locked the door from the inside. So who could it be?

He went out into the hall and opened the door. On the steps stood the bookseller who had given him the Advent calendar!

'Ah, there you are,' he said. 'Just as I thought.'

'Why?' asked Joachim, suddenly a little scared in case the bookseller had come to ask for the magic Advent calendar back. Besides, how did he know where they lived?

The bookseller put his hand into his coat pocket and took out a driving licence.

'Your father left this behind on the counter,' he explained. 'I thought it must be yours, but since you didn't come back to the shop I looked up your name in the telephone directory and found out where you lived. I live hereabouts myself, you see, at number 12 Clover Road.'

That wasn't far. One of Joachim's classmates lived at number 7.

'And how's it going with the magic Advent calendar?' asked the bookseller.

'Great,' said Joachim. 'There are some pieces of paper in it, too.'

'Are there?' said the bookseller, and gave him a big smile. 'Well, I must be getting on,' he said. 'It's a busy time for us booksellers.'

Joachim had decided not to say anything about the driving

licence until Papa mentioned it himself. Instead he started to talk about something completely different.

'What's a pilgrimage?'

'A pilgrim is someone who travels to a holy place,' said Papa, helping himself to more fish pie.

'Like Sigurd Jorsalfar?' continued Joachim. 'He travelled all the way to Jerusalem, didn't he? That's why he was called the traveller to Jerusalem.'

Mama and Papa looked at one another.

'Have you been learning about Sigurd Jorsalfar at school?' asked Mama.

Joachim shook his head. He decided to tell Papa about the driving licence after all.

'Have you found your driving licence yet, Papa?'

'Not a sign,' said Papa crossly.

'But I have,' said Joachim.

He went into his room to fetch the driving licence and handed it to Papa.

Papa nearly choked on his dinner. 'Where did you find it, Joachim? Surely *you* didn't –'

'You left it in the bookshop when we bought the Advent calendar.'

Papa looked as if he had had a visitation from an angel in broad daylight. He had in a way, too, except that the angel had sent a white-haired bookseller instead of coming himself.

'He came here before you got home,' explained Joachim. 'He said he'd looked in the telephone directory.'

Then Mama and Papa realised what had happened.

'Well, he's quite a bookseller,' said Papa. He turned to Mama. 'Quite unusual, you know.'

'And you're quite an unusual muddlehead,' said Joachim.

the
FIFTH
OF DECEMBER

... it's a very unusual way of travelling ...

JOACHIM WAS GLAD there were no chocolates or plastic figures in the old Advent calendar. But Papa had not been quite right when he had said there were only small pictures behind the doors.

A strange story was hidden inside the magic Advent calendar. It would take twenty-four days to read the whole of the tale, since the story was chopped up into twenty-four small chapters, one for each day. Each day another pilgrim joined the pilgrimage.

The fifth of December was a Saturday. Mama and Papa usually slept longer on Saturdays. Joachim woke up at seven as he always did. He sat up in bed and examined the big picture on the outside of the calendar.

Only now did he discover that one of the shepherds was holding a crook in his hand – just like Joshua.

Why hadn't he noticed that before?

Every time he looked at the magic calendar he discovered something new. But surely there couldn't be anything *more* to see than what had been there all the time? Wouldn't that be like a conjuring trick? Perhaps that was what made the old Advent calendar magical? The picture outside had never been completely finished, but it gradually painted in what was missing as somebody opened the doors and read the scraps of paper.

Was it really possible to make a picture like that?

Joachim knew that bread was not quite ready until it had stood and risen all by itself – first on the baking tray and then in the oven. He knew that it had something to do with yeast, for Joachim had often helped his mother or father bake bread. When he was smaller he used to think that babies inside their mothers must be like small pieces of yeast.

Wasn't the whole world a magic picture which added to itself? For the world changed all the time. It was never completely finished.

If God had made a whole world that could create itself in every tiny nook and cranny, could he not then manage to make a picture that developed itself in front of the eyes of those looking at it?

Joachim opened the door with the number 5 on it. Today's picture was of a rowing boat. In the boat there sat a shepherd, an angel, a little girl and several sheep. Joachim knew who they were, but what interested him most was the little scrap of paper.

He unfolded it and began to read.

THE THIRD SHEEP

ELISABET, THE LAMB, the angel, the sheep and the shepherd sped through Sweden along dirt roads and grassy cart tracks, between yellow fields and through dense forests until they looked out over a little town by the sea. The wind was blowing in from the sea so strongly that the waves were breaking over the edge of the quay. Far out on the sea there was a sailing ship with three tall masts. At the edge of the town stood a large castle.

'We are in Halland,' said the angel Ephiriel. 'The town is called Halmstad, and the waves are rolling in from the Kattegat. The watch says that 1789 years have passed since Jesus was born.'

'Are we still in Sweden?' asked Elisabet.

Ephiriel nodded. 'But not so very long ago it was part of Denmark.'

Joshua the shepherd said they should hurry on, and they crossed a landscape that became flatter and flatter the further south they came. Between grazing land and enclosed pastures the countryside revealed small villages, each with a little church and a few houses.

They were rushing through dense woodland when Joshua stopped and knelt under a birch tree. He had found a sheep caught in a snare.

'The snare was probably set for a hare or a fox,' he said, loosening a cord from the sheep's leg. 'But now the sheep can come with us to Bethlehem.'

'It's one of us too,' said Ephiriel.

And the sheep seemed to answer. 'Meh!' it bleated. 'Me-e-eh.'

Off they went again: the lamb and the two sheep first, the shepherd behind them, Elisabet and Ephiriel last.

They entered a town and stopped in front of an old church with two tall towers above the entrance.

The angel told them that they were in Scania, that the town was called Lund and that the big church was an ancient cathedral. He looked at his angel watch and said, 'The watch says 1745. That proud cathedral has stood here for centuries. Churches and cathedrals have been built all over the world, and it all started with the Christ-child who was born in Bethlehem. It's as if a tiny seed of corn is put into the ground and grows into a whole field. The glory of heaven is dispersed very easily.'

Elisabet wondered about what the angel had said.

'Can we go in?' she asked.

The angel nodded, and they went into the great church: the sheep first, the shepherd next, and Elisabet after the shepherd.

Inside was the most beautiful sound Elisabet had ever heard. From the great organ there swelled such rich and powerful melodies that tears came to her eyes.

When the angel saw it, he said, 'Yes, weep, my child. That wonderful music was composed by Johann Sebastian Bach. He is alive in Germany at this time, and his music will be heard throughout Europe. That's not surprising, for his music is like a tiny shred of the glory of heaven.'

The only things that disturbed the music were two sheep bleating and a lamb scurrying about so that its little bell was tinkling.

A man in black robes came towards them from the chancel. It was the priest.

'Get out, all of you!' he said sternly. 'Lund Cathedral is not a common sheepfold.'

Then the angel Ephiriel stepped in front of the priest. He spread out his wings and said, 'The pastor should not be dismayed! Rather, he should not forget that Jesus was born in a stable, and that He was called the "Good Shepherd".'

The priest stopped abruptly, for even though he was a priest in an ancient cathedral, he was not used to angels. He fell to his knees and folded his hands.

'Glory to God in the highest!' he exclaimed.

They left him like that. The angel made a sign to the others that they should go.

'Moments like that should never last too long,' he said. 'He may write a report to the bishop. Then the whole thing will be hushed up, or rumours will start to circulate about the miracle at Lund. In any case the bishop should remind the pastor that the word "pastor" means shepherd, neither more nor less.'

Joshua struck his crook against the church wall.

'To Bethlehem! To Bethlehem!'

They sped through a large park teeming with birds. A couple of soldiers came riding in their direction. When they caught sight of the lively procession, they called out, 'Halt!' and galloped towards them. But just as they bent down from their horses to seize Joshua the shepherd, the soldiers vanished like dew in sunshine.

Elisabet gaped, for they were still standing on the same spot as before the soldiers had ridden up.

'They've disappeared!' she exclaimed.

The angel's laugh was like rippling water.

'Yes, in a way. But *we* were the ones who disappeared. Perhaps they were so terrified when they saw what happened that they fell off their horses.'

Elisabet was still wondering at this, so Ephiriel had to explain to her again how they were travelling.

'We're travelling in two directions at once. One journey goes south on the map to the town of Bethlehem in Judea. The other passes through history to David's city at the time when Jesus was born. It's a very unusual way of travelling; many people would say it was quite impossible, but nothing is impossible for God.'

Elisabet marvelled at the angel's words, and hid them in her heart.

'It makes it simpler to avoid danger,' remarked Joshua. 'If

we can't give the slip to priests or soldiers by taking a step to one side, we have to take a step backwards in time instead. A mere quarter or half an hour can be sufficient.'

With those words they went on their way again. They passed large fields and small villages. Soon they could glimpse the sea in the distance. In a short while they were standing on a deserted beach.

'This is Øre Sound,' said Ephiriel. 'My watch shows that 1703 years have passed since Jesus was born. We must get across to Denmark before the seventeenth century is over.'

'Here's a rowing boat,' announced Joshua.

They climbed on board the boat, the sheep first, Elisabet and Ephiriel behind them. Joshua pushed the boat out and jumped on board at the last minute.

The angel Ephiriel rowed, so strongly that the spray foamed about the prow. The boat was rocked by the waves so that the lamb's bell rang piercingly all the way across.

Joshua sat in the stern. Suddenly he pointed forwards and said, 'I can see Denmark.'

'I CAN SEE Denmark.'

Joachim thought he could see a little of Denmark too, but it was only inside his head.

It was extraordinary that Elisabet was able to travel backwards in time, strange to think that two thousand years had passed since Jesus was born. But the stories about Jesus had travelled through those two thousand years so that Joachim had heard about Him too. In a way Elisabet was travelling in the other direction.

When Mama and Papa got up they had to see the picture in the Advent calendar. Joachim pointed to the boat with Elisabet, Ephiriel, Joshua and the three sheep, but he said nothing about what had happened in the park, or in the cathedral in Lund. They would only have begun to ask how he knew what a cathedral was, and Joachim had decided *not* to talk about the pieces of paper in the calendar. He had hidden them in the secret box.

After breakfast they went to the big department store in town to do some Christmas shopping. In the toy department on the first floor Joachim began to wonder if this was where Elisabet had run after the lamb. There was even an old escalator here. But wasn't it all a very long time ago?

'This shop must be forty years old,' he said to his mother.

She looked at him oddly. 'I should think it's even older than that,' was all she said.

So he found out. Elisabet and the lamb *had* perhaps escaped from this shop. He could understand very well why, for Joachim didn't like shopping in large stores either. He got really angry with the nagging sound of all the cash registers.

That Saturday was extra long because he was thinking about what would happen when Elisabet and the angel Ephiriel got to Denmark. It was even worse at bedtime. He had to lie right under the magic calendar which was still full to bursting with secrets. To sleep so close to all those secrets was like living in a chocolate shop without being allowed to taste one single tiny chocolate.

the
SIXTH
OF DECEMBER

... a camel can move from place to place as well, a bit like the castles on a chessboard ...

WHEN JOACHIM WOKE up on Sunday morning it felt as if he had just fallen asleep, for he hadn't woken once during the whole of that long night. Then he realised that he had dreamed, and as soon as he remembered the dream it seemed to him that the night had been quite a long one after all.

He had dreamt that the magic Advent calendar was filled with small chocolate figures that turned into real animals as soon as he opened the doors and let them out of prison. To stop them running away he had to lock them up in his secret box, and he had only let them out on Christmas Eve. Then all twenty-four chocolate animals crept out through the window and set off through the countryside. They were going to Bethlehem, to Bethlehem – because that's where the Christ-child was born. Joachim knew that Jesus had loved everyone, but in his dream he had been fond of chocolate too.

Joachim sat up and laughed. He was ready to open the sixth door in the Advent calendar. Today there was a picture of a round tower. He would look more closely at the picture afterwards. First he had to read what was on the scrap of paper.

CASPAR

WHEN THE BOAT with Elisabet, the angel Ephiriel, Joshua the shepherd, and the three sheep touched land on the Danish side of the Øre Sound, they were welcomed politely by a black man.

It was Elisabet who discovered him first. The angel, who was rowing, sat with his back to the shore and Joshua was busy keeping the sheep quiet.

'There's a man over there,' she remarked.

The angel glanced over his shoulder and said, 'Then he's one of us.'

The black man had a dark cloak with gold buttons, red woollen trousers, and sheepskin shoes. He came towards them, seized the boat and pulled them up on land. The sheep jumped out first, and soon they were all standing on the beach.

The man with the fine clothes bent down and took Elisabet's hand.

'Greetings to you, my child, and welcome. I am King Caspar of Nubia.'

'Elisabet,' said Elisabet, curtseying politely.

She wasn't quite sure how to behave. Perhaps she should have said that her name was Elisabet Hansen and that she came from Norway, but that wouldn't have been very interesting just after he had told her that he was the King of Nubia.

'He's one of the Three Wise Men from the East,' whispered Ephiriel solemnly.

'Or one of the Three Kings of the Orient,' nodded Joshua.

None of this made the situation any easier for Elisabet. If she was going to say anything, it would have to be that she was the Princess of Toten or something like that. Then maybe the King would have believed that Toten was a mighty kingdom.

The black king bowed again and said, 'The pleasure is on my side of Øre Sound. You should know that I've been standing here waiting for you for so long that between 1701 and 1699 I had to play hopscotch.'

This sounded so mysterious that Elisabet began rubbing her eyes to find out whether she was properly awake. It was difficult enough to play hopscotch between squares on the asphalt, but how could the Wise Man manage to play hopscotch between two different years?

He explained in more detail.

'When I arrived on this shore in the year of Our Lord 1701, some fishermen appeared, and they were so dismayed when they saw one of the Three Wise Men that I had to take a step backwards. That's how I got to the year 1700. I sat down and looked out over Øre Sound, but after a while a couple of soldiers on horseback came from the fortress in Copenhagen. They, too, were somewhat dismayed to see a black king. You see, at the moment I am the only black man in the whole of Denmark, at least, the only one who is a King of the Orient besides. That sort of thing attracts attention, my friends, for people find it difficult to get used to something completely different. So I hurried back to the year 1699, and since then I have waited here. From that time on I have met neither man nor beast, and I have had no need to hide myself from sun and moon, nor from the stars of heaven either, for the stars are so close to God that they would never permit themselves to gossip about the life of humans on earth.'

Elisabet wasn't sure that she understood all this, but she

did see that she was talking to a real wise man. He was so wise that she didn't quite know where to look.

It was a great relief to her when at last the shepherd thumped his crook on the ground.

'To Bethlehem! To Bethlehem!'

The little procession of pilgrims began to move off again: the three sheep first, Joshua and Caspar the black king next, Elisabet and Ephiriel last.

They leapt along broad cobbled streets, and Ephiriel explained that this was Copenhagen, the King's city. It was so early in the morning that the streets were almost deserted. Elisabet thought it was a blessing to see a big city empty of cars. Instead, you had to put up with the horse droppings that were fertilising the streets.

'The time is 1648,' announced the angel Ephiriel. 'It's the last year of Christian the Fourth's reign. He became King of Denmark and Norway when he was still a small child many years ago. Norway is part of Denmark at this time. Christian the Fourth is very fond of Norway and has visited the country often.'

Soon they arrived at the very centre of the Danish capital. They stopped in front of a church with a round tower at one end.

'That's the Round Tower which King Christian has just built on to the new Trinity Church,' said Ephiriel. 'The church towers look imposing, but he thought it was a pity that they should stand there to no purpose. So the Round Tower has been built both as a church tower and as a watch-tower where astronomers can stand in peace and quiet study-ing the movements of the planets and the positions of the stars in the sky. These are the days when the first telescopes are being invented.'

'That's a strange mixture,' said Elisabet.

She felt that she had to say something clever every now and again, but the Wise Man shook his head.

'The stars are created by God, too,' he said. 'So studying the stars in the sky can be like a whole church service. But here they have neither deserts nor camels.'

Elisabet stared at him, puzzled, and the Wise Man continued.

'The best way to study the stars, in the opinion of all Wise Men, is to sit on the back of a camel in the desert. It's almost like sitting in a tower, but a camel can move from place to place as well, a bit like the castles on a chessboard. The only thing that's inconvenient for a camel is to go through the eye of a needle.'

Elisabet was not at all sure whether she agreed that the back of a camel could be compared with a church tower, or a desert with a chessboard.

'The drawback of a watchtower,' Caspar went on, 'is that it usually stands stock still. I've seen a tower that has stood in the same spot for more than a thousand years. The old walls must get bored with the view. On the other hand they have experienced how people have come and gone, and perhaps that has given them insight.'

Elisabet nodded. Caspar had even more to tell her.

'There are two ways of becoming wise. One way is to travel out into the world and to see as much as possible of God's creation. The other is to put down roots in one spot and to study everything that happens there in as much detail as you can. The trouble is that it's impossible to do both at the same time.'

Elisabet was struck with wonder at the Wise Man's words. To be on the safe side she clapped her hands, and the angel and the shepherd did the same. Caspar was infected by their enthusiasm, and began clapping too, because he was so pleased with all that had been said. Elisabet thought it must be fun to keep thinking such clever thoughts.

It was as if the Wise Man had read her thoughts. He said, 'Thinking clever thoughts is almost like being at a circus – not a circus with clowns or elephants, but a real thinking circus. But let it be said once and for all: I am grateful to all clowns and elephants for their attention.'

Joshua thumped his crook on the cobbles.

'To Bethlehem!' he said. 'To Bethlehem!'

The procession of pilgrims began to move along the streets again. Through the city and out to the country they went, between swaying fields of corn and cool, leafy woodland. Denmark seemed to be extra flat: she could see no tall buildings. The only things that pointed upwards occasion-ally were the churches they passed, all of them built in honour of a little child who once upon a time was born in Bethlehem.

They caught sight of the sea in the distance and came down to a small town called Korsør which lay beside the Great Belt, the broad sound between Sjaelland and Fyn.

The people in the town almost fell over when they caught a glimpse of the astonishing procession, but their terror lasted only a short time, for the next moment the procession had moved one or two weeks backwards in the history of the town. Then there were other people who caught a glimpse of the pilgrimage for a second or two. At that time there was continual talk of angels.

Joshua pointed to a large rowing boat at the water's edge.

'We shall have to borrow that,' he said. 'Hurry up now.

It's nearly 1600 years after Jesus's birth.' And he fell to chasing his sheep on board.

Elisabet felt she had to ask whether this wasn't stealing, but Ephiriel reminded her that Jesus had to borrow an ass when he rode into Jerusalem.

A little later they were out on the Great Belt. The angel rowed with one oar, the black king Caspar with the other. He had to work hard in order to row as strongly as Ephiriel.

WHEN MAMA CAME in to look at the Advent calendar, Joachim forgot that he mustn't talk about what he had read on the folded piece of paper. She leaned over the picture.

'That must be the Tower of Babylon.'

Joachim shook his head. 'Oh no. That's the Round Tower in Copenhagen.'

Mama looked at him in astonishment. 'Who told you that?'

'No idea,' replied Joachim. That was how Mama answered him when he asked her something she couldn't tell him. 'It's impossible to play chess with a tower like that, because it stands stock still. And if you sit inside it you soon get bored with the view. But on the other hand you may get some insight.'

Mama clasped her hands together. Joachim thought it was because he had said something clever, but all she said was, 'But Joachim. Where do you *get* all this from?'

the
SEVENTH
OF DECEMBER

... in heaven we've always considered this

to be a slight exaggeration ...

ALL THAT AFTERNOON Joachim kept on thinking about Caspar, the black king who had been waiting in Denmark for Elisabet, the angel Ephiriel, and Joshua the shepherd.

How did he know they were coming? Did Ephiriel and the King of Nubia have an agreement to meet precisely there in the year 1699? There was nothing to show that their meeting was accidental, after all. 'Then he's one of us,' the angel had said as soon as he saw Caspar.

All of a sudden Joachim thought of the bookseller. He had said that the Advent calendar looked home-made, and Joachim agreed. It looked as if it had been cut out and glued at home in the kitchen.

If John had made the magic Advent calendar, he would have been certain to call the girl in the story after Elisabet in the picture. But why had he done it? Why had he made the calendar in order to leave it in a bookshop without knowing what would become of it afterwards?

In the evening, when Joachim was going to bed, he tried to push all the open doors shut again so that he could look at the large picture properly. Then it happened again, and this time with one of the Three Wise Men who were kneeling behind the baby Jesus in the manger. His skin was dark, just like Caspar the black king, and Joachim hadn't noticed it before!

Why hadn't he discovered that?

Again he had the feeling that the picture became clearer and clearer with every day that passed.

Before he put out the light he glanced at it one more time, and thought it must be strange to be in Bethlehem exactly at the time when Jesus was born. Elisabet was on her way there, and in a way he was going along on the journey himself.

When he woke up the next morning he opened the seventh door and saw a picture of a sheep eating grass in front of some high walls. He picked up a scrap of paper that was folded over and over, and read what was written on it.

THE FOURTH SHEEP

THE ANGEL EPHIRIEL and the black king Caspar had rowed Elisabet, Joshua, and the three sheep over the Great Belt.

'We're going ashore again,' said Ephiriel. 'This island is called Fyn, and it's exactly 1599 years since Jesus was born in Bethlehem.'

From the sea they ran towards a large castle on a mound between ramparts and ditches. 'That's Nyborg Castle,' the angel told them. 'We're standing in front of the oldest royal fortress in Scandinavia.'

Elisabet pointed up at one of the ramparts.

'There's a sheep.'

The angel nodded. 'Then it's one of us.'

With that they all leapt up on to the ramparts, the three

sheep first, Joshua and Caspar after them, Elisabet and Ephiriel last.

A soldier rushed out from between the buildings in the castle. He raised a spear and shouted, 'Sheep thieves!'

The next moment three or four soldiers came storming up. All of them had spears and one of them had a kind of gun as well. The angel Ephiriel confronted the soldiers and they threw themselves down on the ground and hid their heads in their hands.

'Fear not!' said the angel in a gentle voice. 'I bring you tidings of great joy. This sheep will come with us to the Holy Land where the Christ-child is to be born.'

Only one of the soldiers dared to look up. He was the one who had called them sheep thieves.

'Be merciful unto us and take the sheep with you,' he cried.

The sheep in question had already joined the others as if it belonged to the little flock. Joshua struck his crook against the rampart and said, 'To Bethlehem! To Bethlehem!'

Off they went across the green island, the four sheep first, Joshua, Caspar, Ephiriel and Elisabet following them.

On the bank of a small river they passed a town with narrow streets and one-storey dwellings. On the outskirts stood an ancient stone church with a square tower.

'That's Odense Cathedral,' said Ephiriel. 'It's called after Canute the Holy who was killed here in the year 1086.'

'What's the time by the angel watch?' asked Elisabet.

'It's 1537 years after Christ. From now on the Bible will be printed in all the languages of the world so that everyone can read about Jesus, for in these days the art of printing will be invented. Before this books have had to be written by hand, and only the priests were able to read the Bible.

But not many people have learned to read. Now it will be decided that everyone must go to school.'

'Some years ago,' said Caspar, 'a Polish astronomer called Copernicus discovered that the earth is as round as a ball and moves in orbit round the sun. This wasn't news to wise men, but to most people it was new and exciting. Sailors could now travel round the world, and that's how Columbus reached America in the year 1492. After him the Spanish sailors cruelly attacked the Indians. In the opinion of the Kings of the Orient it would have been better if they had kept to the ships of the desert, for there is no more peaceful animal than a camel in the desert, and peace is the message of Christmas.'

Elisabet was still trying to understand what the Wise Man had said when Joshua struck the ground with his crook.

'To Bethlehem! To Bethlehem!'

They went on their way along a ridge that gave them a good view over Fyn. Now and then they looked down on a horse drawing a plough or an ox harnessed to a cart.

'It's not so flat here,' said Elisabet as she ran. 'But we're still in Denmark, aren't we?'

The angel nodded. 'Yes indeed, and the Danes are very proud of ridges like this, but we're only a hundred metres above sea level. They have called the hillsides we can see down there on the left the Fyn Alps. Another ridge is called the Heavenly Mountain. In heaven we've always considered this to be a slight exaggeration.'

The procession had paused, and Caspar joined in the conversation again.

'But it's important to be happy about the little you have. However little it is, it's infinitely more than nothing.'

'If the world was as round and smooth as a ball,' said

Elisabet thoughtfully, 'there wouldn't be one single mountain on the whole earth. But then, even a rocky slope would be as exciting as the highest mountain in Norway, as long as it was the only rocky slope.'

'So, you see how easily clever ideas travel,' said the Wise Man. 'You've been with a Wise Man for only a fairly short time, but you've already understood a tiny part of the heavenly wisdom. Bravo!'

Elisabet was glad she had said something clever for once. She felt so cheered by it that she tried again.

'And if the world was as small as the moon, nobody would have complained that it hadn't been made a bit larger.'

'How true that is,' said Caspar. 'Even if the world had been no larger than a pea, it would have been as big a mystery. For where would the little pea have come from? That too would have had to be created by God. It's no easier to create a pea than to create a whole solar system.'

Elisabet thought this was a bit of an exaggeration, for if the world hadn't been any larger than a pea, it wouldn't have had room for even Adam and Eve.

'If there had been only one star in the sky,' Caspar continued, 'that one star would have aroused as much wonder as all the other stars together. After all, nobody goes round complaining because there's only one moon. On the contrary: if there had been a hundred moons they would only have got in each other's way. So the creation of billions of stars in the sky was an excessive exaggeration. Whenever there's too much of anything, you can stare at it without appreciating it. That's how it's possible to be out under a starry sky and fail to see a single star because of a shower of shooting stars.'

It was quite true, thought Elisabet. She had often looked

at a sky full of stars without finding any particular one.

Caspar went on, 'In the opinion of the Kings of the Orient, God spoiled humans a bit, because He created far too much at the same time. He created so many strange things to look at that many people don't see God. But that's how he managed to hide Himself too. He wouldn't have been able to do that if only four people, three trees, two sheep and eight camels existed in the whole of creation. If only one fish could be found in the sea, people would probably have noticed how perfect it was. And then they might have started asking who had made it.'

For a while he remained standing, looking about him. Elisabet thought he was waiting for someone to applaud his wise words, so she clapped her hands together. Then the others began clapping as well.

'There, there,' said Caspar. 'That wasn't so much to clap for.'

Then he seemed to change his mind.

'Although it was infinitely more than nothing.'

The procession of pilgrims ran down towards a little town beside a narrow strip of water.

'The sound is called the Little Belt,' said Ephiriel. 'The time is 1504 years after Christ.'

Before Elisabet was able to ask how they were going to cross the sound, Joshua was on his way towards a boat that lay moored to a little quay. In the boat sat a young man drawing up a fishing line. When he caught sight of the angel Ephiriel he dropped the line into the sea and threw himself down with his head on the deck.

'Be not afraid,' said Ephiriel. 'We are pilgrims on our way to the Holy Land where Jesus is to be born. Can you row us over the Little Belt?'

'Amen,' replied the ferryman. 'Amen, amen...'

The angel knew his answer meant yes. The four sheep and the rest of the pilgrims climbed on board the boat.

While the ferryman rowed across the sound he stared and stared at Ephiriel. It was probably the first time he had seen a proper angel. He didn't even glance at the black king, Caspar.

If the angel had not been with them, Elisabet thought, the ferryman would most certainly have had more than enough to do, staring at the black king. Only if the king had not been with them either, would he perhaps have looked at her. She thought it was a shame that the world should be like that.

When they were over on the other side and the sheep began jumping out of the boat, they said thank you and goodbye to the ferryman. As for the ferryman, he only repeated what he had already said over and over again. 'Amen, amen...'

JOACHIM HAD JUST finished reading what was on the paper when his mother came into the room. He screwed up the paper quickly, but Mama saw that he was hiding something.

'What are you holding in your hand?'

'Nothing,' he said. 'Only air.'

'May I see it, then?'

But Joachim held the ball of paper so hard that his knuckles were quite white.

'It's a Christmas present,' he said.

The words 'Christmas present' might have been magic. At any rate they made Mama smile broadly.

'For me?'

Joachim nodded.

'Then I won't look,' said Mama. 'But it must be a very tiny Christmas present.'

'It's infinitely bigger than nothing,' said Joachim.

So Mama went to the bathroom.

Joachim thought it was strange that everything that had to do with Christmas was so special. It was one of the most secret things in the whole world.

But Mama was mistaken about one thing. What he was holding in his hand wasn't a *tiny* Christmas present.

the
EIGHTH
OF DECEMBER

. . . part of the glory of heaven that has

strayed down to earth . . .

ON THE EIGHTH of December Joachim was woken by Mama. She ruffled his hair and said, 'Time to get up, Joachim. It's half past seven, and you start school early today.'

He drew himself up in bed. The first thing he thought of was the magic Advent calendar hanging above his head.

Mama seemed to read his thoughts. 'But you have time to open the Advent calendar.'

Joachim thought quickly. He thought so quickly that there was room for an awful lot of thoughts before Mama went on, 'Aren't you going to open it, then? I'd like to see it too.'

No! thought Joachim. He *couldn't* open the magic Advent calendar while Mama was watching

'I don't think you're properly awake yet,' Mama went on. 'Perhaps you'll let me open the Advent calendar today?'

'No!' said Joachim, so loudly and clearly that Mama jumped. 'I'll wait till I come home from school. I'll have more time then.'

He jumped out of bed quickly to be quite certain Mama wasn't going to start opening the calendar.

'Of course you do just as you like,' she said.

She went out to the kitchen while Joachim got dressed.

When Joachim came home from school a man he did not recognise was standing outside the garden gate. Since he didn't know the man, Joachim pretended he hadn't seen him. He opened the gate and closed it after him.

'Is your name Joachim?' asked the stranger.

Joachim stopped on the path that Papa had almost cleared of snow and turned towards the man. He was quite old; he looked kind too. Joachim didn't like someone he didn't know to know his name, but he had to answer.

'Yes,' he said. 'That's me.'

The man nodded. He came right up to the gate and leaned over it. He was wearing a green felt hat.

'I thought so.' He had rather an odd accent. Perhaps he wasn't Norwegian.

'You've been given a fine Advent calendar, haven't you?'

Joachim gave a start. How did he know that?

'A magic Advent calendar,' answered Joachim.

'A magic Advent calendar, yes. Price: 75 øre. My name's John. I sell flowers at the market.'

Joachim stood stock still without saying anything. In his Advent calendar he had read about people who had suddenly seen an angel; now it was almost as if he was being visited by an angel himself.

He knew this meeting with the flower-seller was important and he wanted to say something serious, but he only managed, 'How did you know where I lived?'

John chuckled to himself. 'Good question, my boy,' he said. 'I often go into the bookshop, you see. I like it there. I wanted to hear where the old calendar had ended up. It was a good thing your father forgot his driving licence. If he hadn't it would have been much more difficult for me to find you. But I expect you'd have come down to me on the market sooner or later. Don't you think so?'

Joachim nodded. He *had* thought of it. 'Did you know there were some pieces of paper in the Advent calendar?' he asked.

'If there's anyone in the whole world who knows, it must be me. Now you know too,' said John.

'Is it home-made?'

'Completely home-made, yes, and very old. But that's an old story too. Have you opened the calendar today?'

Joachim shook his head. 'I have to do it when Mama and Papa aren't looking, because I don't want them to know about the pieces of paper. I'm going to pack them up on Christmas Eve and put them under the Christmas tree.'

'That's a good idea,' said John. 'But what about yesterday, then? Didn't the pilgrims take a sheep with them from the old castle on Fyn, and the angel Ephiriel had to say "Be not afraid" to the sentries at the castle?'

Joachim was almost scared because John knew all about it.

'Did *you* make the magic Advent calendar?' he asked.

'Yes and no . . .'

Joachim was afraid he might go, so he quickly asked another question.

'Did it all really happen, or did you make it up?'

John looked serious. 'It's all right to ask, but it isn't always so easy to answer.'

Joachim said, 'I wondered whether Elisabet in the magic Advent calendar was the same as the Elisabet whose picture was in the bookshop.'

'So he told you about the old picture too?' said John, sighing heavily. 'Well, well, I have nothing to hide any more,

I'm too old for that now. But it isn't Christmas yet, so we'd better talk about Elisabet another time.'

He took a step back. 'Sabet ... tebas ...' he mumbled to himself. Joachim didn't understand that, but perhaps he hadn't been meant to hear it.

Finally John said, 'I must go now. But we'll meet again, for that old story links us human beings together.' He walked away rapidly and soon disappeared.

Joachim was annoyed that he hadn't had time to ask more questions. He ought to have asked whether the big calendar picture was gradually changing as he read the pieces of paper.

He hurried into the house and opened the door with the number 8 on it. Today there was a picture of a shepherd carrying a lamb on his shoulders. Joachim picked up the paper, smoothed it out carefully, and read.

JACOB

O N ONE OF the last days of the year 1499 after Christ four sheep, one shepherd, one King of the Orient, one angel and a little girl from Norway flocked out of a boat that had brought them across the Little Belt to Jutland.

'Thank goodness!' exclaimed Caspar as they stepped on land.

'Yes, it'll be a long time now before we have to do that again,' replied Joshua.

The angel Ephiriel nodded. 'Verily I say unto you that there will be only one more time before we get to Bethlehem.'

Elisabet had no idea what they were talking about. 'Isn't it still terribly far to Bethlehem?' she asked.

'Yes, indeed,' said the angel. 'It is far, and many hundreds of years too. But there is only one more stretch of ocean to cross. That won't happen until we get to the Black Sea.'

The little procession came to a town at the inner end of a fjord. At one end of the town stood a large fortress.

'This town is called Kolding and is in South Jutland,' said the angel Ephiriel. 'It has been an important trading place for hundreds of years. The fortress is called Koldinghaus and the kings of Denmark have often lived here. The time is 1488 years after Christ's birth.'

Joshua struck the ground with his crook.

'To Bethlehem! To Bethlehem!'

They came to the top of a little ridge with fine views over the countryside. Fresh flowers were growing everywhere, so it must have been early summer. Elisabet pointed down at the ground as she ran.

'Look at all the lovely wild flowers!' she said.

The angel nodded mysteriously.

'They are part of the glory of heaven that has strayed down to earth,' he explained. 'You see, there's so much glory in heaven that it can easily spill over.'

Elisabet pondered over the angel's words and hid them in her heart.

Suddenly the shepherd stopped and pointed at the little flock of sheep.

'A lamb is missing!'

He needed to say no more, for all of them saw that the earth seemed to have swallowed up the lamb with the bell.

'Where *is* it?' exclaimed Elisabet.

'The lambs are so charming with their white fleece that

they're a delight to the eye, but they're almost uncontrollable,' said Joshua. 'It doesn't always help to put a bell on them, either. If I'm watching one lamb, the other will suddenly vanish. And when I find the second lamb, all of a sudden the first lamb will decide to leave the flock. Shepherding is a difficult job, and it's especially difficult to herd a flock of sheep all the way to Bethlehem. As it is written, now I must leave the other sheep to look for the one lamb that is missing.'

Elisabet felt her eyes fill with tears. But just then a man appeared over the crest of the ridge. He was wearing clothes exactly like Joshua's and on his shoulders he was carrying the lamb with the bell.

'He is one of us,' said Ephiriel.

The man put the lamb down at Elisabet's feet. He held out his hand to Joshua and said, 'I am Jacob the shepherd and the second of the shepherds in the field. Now I can help care for the flock that's going to Bethlehem.'

Elisabet clapped her hands. Joshua struck the ground with his crook and said, 'To Bethlehem! To Bethlehem!'

The two shepherds ran behind the little flock, with Caspar the black king, the angel Ephiriel and Elisabet behind them.

As they were passing the old market town of Flensburg the angel Ephiriel said, 'The time is 1402 years after the birth of Christ. We shall soon be crossing the frontier into Germany and diving down into the depths of the Middle Ages.'

JOACHIM STOOD LOST in thought. The angel Ephiriel had said that the wild flowers were a part of the glory of heaven that had strayed down to earth, because there's so much glory in heaven that it can easily spill over. Probably only a flower-seller could write something like that.

He didn't tell Mama and Papa that John had visited him. If he told them about that he would have to give away the secret of the scraps of paper too.

Joachim now had so many secrets to keep that he felt his head could split at any moment.

the
NINTH
OF DECEMBER

... they had broken a solemn promise ...

JOACHIM COULDN'T STOP thinking about the words John
had muttered to himself. 'Sabet ... Tebas.'

Who or what were Sabet and Tebas? Could those
strange words have anything to do with the magic
Advent calendar?

Before he went to bed he wrote the words down in a little
notebook so as not to forget them by the morning. Then he
discovered something odd: SABET became TEBAS when he
read it backwards. So of course TEBAS turned into SABET too.

This was so mysterious that he wrote down the two words
like this:

<pre>
        S
        A
T E B A S
        E
        T
</pre>

Perhaps one day the magic words would help him to understand more about the old Advent calendar.

Suddenly he remembered something the bookseller had
said. Hadn't he said that the old flower-seller was a bit odd?
Joachim didn't think he seemed the least bit odd. Of course,
it was unusual to pour water over people's heads, but it was
just the sort of thing that Joachim might suddenly decide to
do himself.

As soon as Joachim woke up on the ninth of December he sat up in bed and hurried to open the Advent calendar. It was a picture of a man playing a pipe. After the man came a long procession of children, big and small.

Joachim looked at it for a long time before he picked up the piece of paper that had fallen out of the calendar. He made himself comfortable and read what was on the paper.

THE FIFTH SHEEP

I T WAS THE year 1378 after Christ. Three godly sheep and a lamb with a bell stormed into the Hanseatic city of Hamburg. Behind the little flock ran two shepherds. An elegantly dressed black king followed the shepherds. Behind the black man a little girl was running as fast as her short legs would carry her. After the girl an angel hovered above the ground.

It was Sunday and early in the morning. A few people were about in the streets on their way to morning mass in the old Jacob Church. As soon as they caught sight of the procession of pilgrims they gestured with their arms. Some of them shaded their eyes, and one of them exclaimed, 'God be praised!'

Something similar had happened in the town of Hanover a few years earlier. It was 1351, immediately after the fearful Plague that had cost so many human lives, not only in Germany, but in the whole of Europe. It was a Monday, and the market stalls on the great market square were about to open. Peasants in their worn, homespun clothes and market women in rough skirts had begun setting out their wares.

All of them had lost some of their dear ones. It was just before the dawn of a new day.

It was then that a little flock of sheep suddenly sprang into the market. One of the sheep overturned a table of vegetables. After the sheep there came a strange company. There were a couple of shepherds, and a man in exotic clothes, black-skinned like an African. The black man was followed by a white-clad figure with wings on its back. Right at the end there appeared a little girl. She stumbled over the shaft of a cart full of cabbages and lay there after the rest of the godly company had left the market.

Elisabet wept bitterly when she saw the angel Ephiriel and all the others disappearing. It was the second time on the long journey south that she had fallen and hurt herself. Now she had lost the procession of pilgrims and was surrounded by people she didn't know. Not only was she in a foreign country, she was in a foreign century too.

The people in the market were terrified by what they had seen. They crowded round Elisabet, and a man poked her with his foot as if he was afraid to touch her. He wrinkled his nose and grunted horribly. But soon an old woman put Elisabet on her feet and tried to comfort her. She spoke a language Elisabet didn't understand.

'I'm going to Bethlehem,' said Elisabet.

And the market woman replied, 'Hamelin? Hamelin?'

'No, no!' sobbed Elisabet. 'To Bethlehem! To Bethlehem!'

Those were her words. The next moment one of the angels of the Lord appeared in an arc of light above the market. Elisabet stretched out her arms towards the angel and cried, 'Ephiriel! Ephiriel!'

The people in the market threw themselves to the ground, but the angel lifted Elisabet up into the air, flew over the spire of the new Market Church, and was gone.

He put her down on a country road outside the town where the sheep, the shepherds, and Caspar the black king were waiting.

'Isn't that just what I was saying?' chuckled Joshua. 'When one of the lambs is lost, the shepherd must leave his flock and find the lamb that has wandered away.'

He struck the ground with his crook. 'To Bethlehem! To Bethlehem!'

'How far is it to Bethlehem?' asked Elisabet.

'Not very far, my dear,' said Ephiriel.

After a while they came to a town on the bank of another river.

'This is Hamelin,' said Ephiriel. 'The river is called the Weser, and the year is 1304 after Jesus's birth. A few years ago a dreadful misfortune occurred in this town. Well, in a way they only had themselves to blame. They had broken a solemn promise, and that's something one should never do.'

'What happened?' asked Elisabet.

'The town had been plagued by rats for a long time. But then a rat-catcher arrived in town. He played on a magic pipe, and the sound of the pipe made all the rats follow him. The piper led the rats to the river, where they all drowned.'

'Wasn't that a good thing?'

'Yes, of course, but the people in the town had promised the man a big reward if he could save them from the plague of rats. When he had rid them of the rats, they refused to pay what they owed him.'

'What did the rat-catcher do then?'

'He began to play on his magic pipe again, and all the children in the town were bewitched by the music of the pipe and followed him. They disappeared inside a huge mountain with the piper, and were never seen again.'

Elisabet realised that maybe the woman in the market at Hanover had thought she was one of the children who had been lured into the mountain by the rat-catcher from Hamelin.

They were about to hurry on through Europe and even further back into history, when a sheep came running towards them along the road and joined the others. Now the flock numbered five sheep.

Joshua struck the ground with his crook.

'To Bethlehem! To Bethlehem!'

JOACHIM FOUND THE key to his box and hid the little piece of paper along with all the other pieces. When his mother came in a little later he was sitting looking at the picture in the Advent calendar.

Mama leaned over him.

'Well, look at that. A piper . . .'

'He's a rat-catcher,' said Joachim. 'They wouldn't give him his reward for taking all the rats away from Hamelin, so he took all the children away with him instead. The people in the town had broken a solemn promise, and that's something one should never do.'

Then his father came in as well. 'What's that you're telling us?' he asked.

Joachim realised that he had forgotten again, and babbled about what he had read on the piece of paper.

'I'm just making it up,' he said. 'It's only something I'm inventing.'

'No, it isn't, Joachim,' said Papa firmly. 'You were talking about the Pied Piper of Hamelin. That's an old story from Germany. Who told you about that?'

What could he say? He had to hit on something clever.

'Ingvild,' he said. She was his teacher. 'Or maybe it was someone in the class.'

He was telling lies. But wasn't he allowed to lie about a Christmas present? Wasn't that the only thing in the whole world that you could lie about as much as you liked?

After school Mama and Joachim went into town to buy an anorak, and Joachim asked to go into the market.

There were not as many people in the market as there were in summer. Some stallholders were selling wreaths and candles, others were selling all sorts of Christmas presents.

'I wonder how they can bear to stand here in the middle of the winter,' shivered Mama. 'There's someone over there selling flowers, too.'

'That's because part of the glory of heaven has strayed down to earth,' said Joachim. Something was laughing inside him.

'What *are* you talking about?' asked Mama.

'He's selling flowers in the middle of the winter because the glory of heaven has strayed down to earth,' repeated Joachim. 'You see, there's so much glory in heaven that it can easily spill over.'

Mama shook her head and sighed in despair. She obviously didn't like him to say such strange things.

John was standing behind a table with lots of flowers on it. He winked at Joachim and gave a little wave.

When they had passed, Joachim turned round. John was pretending to play on an invisible pipe.

the
TENTH
OF DECEMBER

. . . a few seconds later what Elisabet had thought

was a bird took off and flew down in a spiral towards

the pilgrims . . .

JOACHIM WOKE UP and opened the tenth door in the magic Advent calendar. Today there was a picture of an angel at the top of a church tower. Out of the calendar fell a scrap of paper, folded over and over. Joachim unfolded it and began to read.

IMPURIEL

IT HAPPENED AT Paderborn at the end of the thirteenth century. Into the little town halfway between Hanover and Cologne rushed a frisky flock of sheep, followed by two shepherds, a black king, a little girl and an angel with wings outspread.

It was early in the morning before the town was awake; only a night watchman was out in the streets. He called out sternly to the two shepherds who were chasing their flock of sheep through the town. The next moment he caught sight of the angel hovering above the cobblestones. Then he raised his arms to the sunrise and exclaimed, 'Alleluia! Alleluia!'

Whereupon he retreated round a corner and left the streets to the godly procession.

They stopped in front of a church in the middle of the town.

'That's St Bartholomew's Church,' said Ephiriel. 'It was built in the eleventh century and is called after one of Jesus's twelve apostles. It is told of Bartholomew that he journeyed all the way to India to tell the Indians about Jesus.'

Elisabet had noticed something strange. She pointed up at the spire on the church tower.

'There's a white bird sitting up there,' she said.

Ephiriel smiled. 'If only there were,' he said.

A few seconds later, what Elisabet had thought was a bird took off and flew down in a spiral towards the pilgrims. She realised that the bird wasn't a bird after all. What had been sitting on the church spire was an angel. But it was not a grown angel: it was no larger than she was herself.

The child angel alighted at Elisabet's feet.

'Wonderful!' he exclaimed. 'My name is Impuriel and I'm coming with you to Bethlehem.'

He whirled around a bit, peered up at Caspar and the two shepherds, then looked up at Ephiriel and said, 'I've been waiting for a quarter of an eternity.'

Caspar stood thinking. It was obvious he had something on his mind.

'A quarter of an eternity,' he began. 'That's about 66,289 years ... or about 156,498 years ... or more exactly, 439 million 811 thousand 977 years and 4 seconds ... or perhaps even a little more. It's not easy to say how long a quarter of an eternity lasts. First you have to find out how long a *whole* eternity lasts, then you have to divide it by four, but exactly how long a whole eternity lasts is very difficult to calculate. No matter which number you start with, eternity will last even longer. So one can say that a quarter of an eternity is as long as a whole eternity. Even a thousandth of an eternity is really just as long as the whole of the rest of eternity. This is extremely difficult to understand, for calculating whole or half eternities is a matter for heaven alone.'

The angel Impuriel looked offended. 'But I've been sitting on top of the church tower for *hours*,' he said.

'Very possibly, but that's not the same as sitting there for a quarter of an eternity,' said Caspar.

To avoid a quarrel between the Wise Man and the cherub, and not just a quarter of a quarrel, Joshua struck the cobblestones with his crook, and said, 'To Bethlehem! To Bethlehem!'

They set off through the town and out along roads and cattle trails. Impuriel sprang in front of the five sheep, so the pilgrimage was guarded by angels at both ends.

They saw many towns and villages, but didn't stop until they came to the old Roman colonial city of Cologne on the bank of the River Rhine. Ephiriel had explained that their route through Europe had been planned so that they should be seen by as few people as possible.

'Angel time says it's 1272 years after Christ,' he said. 'They've begun building the great cathedral of Cologne, but it won't be finished for hundreds of years.'

Joshua banged with his crook: 'To Bethlehem! To Bethlehem!'

Impuriel said, 'Glorious countryside, isn't it? We're going up the Rhine Valley. There are fortresses and castles, steep vineyards and Gothic cathedrals, dandelions and rhubarb.'

They hurried along the bank of the biggest river Elisabet had ever seen. The valley became narrower and narrower and the mountains higher and higher. They ran past small towns and villages. Out on the river floated an occasional barge.

As they sped through the beautiful landscape, Elisabet turned towards Ephiriel and asked whether he had met Impuriel before.

'All the angels in heaven have known each other through all eternity,' said Ephiriel, laughing.

'Are there an awful lot of you?'

'Yes, a whole host.'

'How can you all know each other, then?'

'We've had the whole of eternity to get to know each other, and you see, that's a very long time.'

Elisabet had to think hard so as to understand what Ephiriel meant. The angel explained a bit more.

'If you have a party that lasts for three hours, you shouldn't invite more than five or six guests, and then everyone will be able to talk to everyone else. But if the party lasts for three whole days, you can easily have fifty or more guests.'

Elisabet nodded. She had discussed this with Mama when it was her birthday.

'So?' she said.

'The heavenly party has lasted for all eternity,' said Ephiriel.

'Do all the angels have different names?'

'Of course. Otherwise we couldn't call out to each other. Otherwise we wouldn't have been *persons* either.'

And Ephiriel began to say all the angel names, one after the other.

'The angels in heaven are called Ariel, Beriel, Curruciel, Daniel, Ephiriel, Fabiel, Gabriel, Hammarubiel, Immanuel, Joachiel, Chachaduriel, Luxuriel, Michael, Narriel . . .'

'That's enough!' said Elisabet. 'How long would it take you to say *all* the angel names?'

'I would have to go on for all eternity.'

'That's pretty good going, to remember all the names by heart,' said Elisabet.

'With all of eternity at your disposal it's not so difficult.'

'And I think it's very clever to think up so many different names all ending in -el,' Elisabet went on.

Ephiriel nodded. 'God's imagination is infinite, just as there are infinitely many stars in the sky. No angel is exactly like another, nor are humans either. You can make a thousand identical machines, but they are so easy to make that even a human can do it.'

Finally the angel Ephiriel spoke some words that Elisabet hid in her heart. 'Every person on earth is a unique work of creation.'

JOACHIM SAT SMILING to himself. It had been such fun to read about all the angels. Suddenly he heard Mama on the landing. He didn't have time to hide the paper in the secret box, so he slipped it under his pillow.

Mama leaned over the bed to peep in the calendar.

'An angel,' she said, 'on a church tower.'

And then something stupid happened. Joachim forgot that he wasn't supposed to talk about what he had read. Perhaps it was because he was trying to remember all those strange angel names. He said, 'That's the cherub Impuriel.'

Mama stared at him. 'Impuriel?'

Joachim nodded. He thought it was a nice name for a mischievous angel, so nice that he kept repeating it inside himself.

'He's sitting on the top of St Bartholomew's church. He's been sitting there for a quarter of an eternity, but now he's about to take off and fly in a spiral down to Elisabet and the others.'

Mama didn't answer Joachim. Instead she called Papa.

When he came into the room she asked Joachim to tell him
what the church in the picture was called.

'St Bartholomew's Church,' he said. 'Bartholomew went
all the way to India and told the Indians about Jesus. But
the church is in Germany, in Paderburg or somewhere.'

Mama and Papa stood staring at each other.

'I'll look it up in the encyclopedia,' said Papa. 'Then we'll
find out.'

When he came back he looked like a ghost, or at least as
if he had met an angel or two on the landing.

'He's quite right. The town's called Paderborn, and there
really is an old St Bartholomew's Church there.'

They were gazing at Joachim just as they had done last
year when he ate nearly all the little Christmas cookies the
day before Christmas Eve.

Papa took the magic Advent calendar down from the wall
and inspected it on both sides. Then he hung it up again.

'And how did you hear about Bartholomew, my lad?' asked
Papa. 'Or about Paderborn for that matter?'

'At school,' said Joachim.

'And you're telling the truth?'

Either you were allowed to tell lies about Christmas presents, or you weren't.

'Yes,' whispered Joachim.

Then they all ran out of time, so there was no more talk
of Bartholomew, Impuriel or Paderborn. Neither Mama nor
Papa had time to make their sandwiches for lunch.

Joachim's most important victory that morning was that
he managed to hide the little piece of paper in his secret box
before he ran off to school. He hid the key in the bookshelf.

When he came home from school, Mama was there. She
had opened his secret box!

*   *   *

She had opened his secret box. Mama had done something she had promised she would never do. She had broken a solemn promise. She had done something that was as bad as opening other people's letters.

On the dining table lay all ten pieces of paper that Joachim had found in the magic Advent calendar.

He was furious. He was so angry with Mama that he wanted to hit her.

'You *promised* me that the secret box was *mine* and that you'd *never* open it,' he said. 'So you tell lies. And you steal too.'

Then Papa came home. He had talked to Mama on the phone. It was he who had said she should try to find the key and open the secret box. They had to find out how Joachim knew so many strange names and used so many grown-up words.

Joachim said they shouldn't have been allowed to have children, for people who tell lies to their children might suddenly begin to hit as well, he said – and *that* was against the law. They could at least have waited until he came home from school and *asked* if they could open his box. Finally he managed to say that he had hidden the scraps of paper because he wanted to pack them up and give them to Mama and Papa for Christmas. He said that he'd throw away the whole of the magic Advent calendar. Then he began to cry. He rushed into his room and slammed the door behind him as hard as he could.

He was *never* going to forgive them! He would *never* listen to them any more either. He would *never* believe them again. Never!

Joachim sat on his bed and tried to look up at the magic Advent calendar, but his eyes were so wet that the colours slid into one another, and he could no longer pick out the angels from the shepherds in the fields. *Everything* was spoilt. The Advent calendar had suddenly become ordinary, like every other Advent calendar. It wasn't the least bit magical any more.

After a long time something began to sing in his ears, and the song he heard was something like: SABET-TEBAS-SABET-TEBAS-SABET-TEBAS . . .

It was such a mysterious song that he suddenly realised that perhaps it didn't make any difference whether Mama and Papa knew about the scraps of paper in the Advent calendar. Perhaps the magic Advent calendar was so full of secrets that there would be enough for the whole family.

He had still not said that he had met John. That was something he had to himself.

There was a knock at the door. Joachim didn't answer, but after a little while Papa cautiously opened the door.

'It's true, we've been silly,' he said.

'Can you forgive us?' asked Mama.

'Did you read what was on the secret pieces of paper?' asked Joachim.

'I suppose I did,' said Mama. 'But you see I don't know which piece came out of the calendar first. Maybe you can show us – and perhaps read it all to Papa?'

Joachim considered carefully.

'All right, then.'

He was a little relieved at what had happened, really. From now on he had no need to hide anything. Besides, he would be able to ask Mama and Papa if there was something he didn't understand.

From now on the magic Advent calendar would belong to the whole family.

the
ELEVENTH
OF DECEMBER

. . . many people are terribly frightened when they

see one of the angels of the Lord . . .

THE REST OF the afternoon was spent poring over the scraps of paper that had fallen out of the magic Advent calendar one after the other. Joachim had tried to put them in the right order, so that Mama and Papa could read the story.

As they read, Papa said, 'That's the strangest thing I've ever seen. We must find out more about this. I wonder how many calendars like this were made . . .'

And Mama kept saying, 'I've never seen anything like it. Imagine bringing home *this* Advent calendar, Joachim!'

When it was evening and Joachim had to go to bed, he sat up for a long time, staring at the calendar. Then it happened again.

IT HAD HAPPENED AGAIN! On the big calendar picture were painted many angels floating down from the sky. Joachim had seen that before. But only today did he discover that one of the angels in the picture was a cherub.

He was quite sure. Impuriel the cherub had not been in the picture until Joachim had read that he flew in spirals down from the tall church tower.

'Mama!' he shouted. 'Papa!'

Both of them came rushing into his room. They were obviously afraid that something dreadful had happened to him. He was a bit shocked himself.

'I can see the angel Impuriel!' was all he said.

Mama and Papa turned to go back. Perhaps they thought he had been visited by an angel, but Joachim asked them to look at the picture carefully.

'Can you see anything you haven't seen before?' he asked.

They leaned over the picture.

Papa said he might not have noticed everything when the bookseller gave them the calendar. He had been so flustered that he had left his driving licence on the counter. For instance, he hadn't noticed that one of the shepherds was holding a shepherd's crook in his hand.

'I don't think I had noticed the little angel either,' remarked Mama.

'Of course not!' said Joachim. 'Because he hasn't been there till now. And that's because it's a magic Advent calendar.'

'Now then, we mustn't exaggerate,' objected Papa. He always liked to seem sensible.

The last thing Joachim thought before he fell asleep was that one of the angels in heaven was called Joachiel – almost the same as himself.

The next morning Joachim opened the eleventh door in the Advent calendar. He had to coax the piece of paper out before he discovered a picture of a horse and rider.

He made himself comfortable under the duvet and read what was on the sheet of paper. Today he had no need to be afraid that Mama or Papa would catch him redhanded, because the secret pieces of paper in the calendar were not secret any more.

BALTHAZAR

FIVE SHEEP, TWO shepherds, two angels, one King of Orient, and a little girl from Norway were speeding up the Valley of the Rhine 1199 years after Jesus was born. They could just glimpse a church tower on the other side of the river. Ephiriel told them it was Mainz Cathedral.

'We have to cross the river,' said Joshua. 'It's a pity, because we shall have to frighten another poor ferryman and explain that we're pilgrims on our way to the Holy Land.'

'We shall have to try to do it gently,' said Ephiriel.

'I can see a boat down there,' exclaimed Impuriel.

He flew high in the air, beating his short wings in the direction of the boat, with the rest of the procession after him, and started talking to a man who was sitting on the river bank.

'Can you row us across? We're going all the way to Bethlehem, and we don't have much time if we're to get there before Jesus is born. We're on a godly errand, you see, so we're not just anybody.'

Ephiriel hurried after him. When he had caught up with Impuriel he nodded apologetically at the ferryman and said to Impuriel, 'How many times do I have to remind you that first of all you must say, "Fear not"?'

But the ferryman, who was unusually and splendidly dressed in a long red cloak, was not scared by the cherub. He turned to Ephiriel and said, 'My name is Balthazar, Second Wise Man and King of Sheba. I'm going the same way as you.'

'Then you are one of us,' said Ephiriel.

All the same, he had to give Impuriel a little scolding.

'This time things fortunately turned out well. But you must always start by saying, "Fear not". Don't you realise that many people are terribly frightened when they see one of the angels of the Lord, at any rate when we beat our wings?'

'Sorry!' said Impuriel.

'All right, all right,' replied Ephiriel.

'But isn't it odd that they should be so frightened just because they've seen an angel?' argued Impuriel. 'I've never so much as harmed a cat. In fact, I couldn't count all the times I've helped a poor cat down from a tall tree. Of course the cats ought to learn once and for all not to climb too high up in the trees, but when we do come and help them, they're not in the slightest bit frightened. It's always humans who are so terribly nervous.'

The two Wise Men had embraced each other.

'It's been a very long time,' said the one .

'And it was a very, very long way from the Rhine,' answered the other.

'But it's very, very, very pleasant to see you again.'

They had their arms round each other, so it was not easy to say who had said what. But now the whole of the pilgrims' procession went on board the boat. The Kings of Orient each took an oar and rowed across the river, which was almost as wide as a stretch of ocean.

On the other side Ephiriel pointed up at the beautiful cathedral. It seemed a little dumpy and hadn't such a tall tower as many of the other churches they had passed, but it was much older.

'The year is 1186 after Christ. Work on this cathedral began more than two hundred years ago. At that time almost a thousand years had passed since the one seed was sown in the earth so that a field of churches and cathedrals should grow over the whole world.'

'A whole field of churches!' repeated Impuriel. 'It would be fun to work out how many kilos of stone and timber have been used to celebrate Jesus's birth, not to mention how many cakes have been baked or how many parcels have been packed. Christmas is the world's biggest birthday party, for everybody in the whole world is invited to join in. That's why the party has lasted for so many years.'

Joshua struck the ground with his crook.

'To Bethlehem! To Bethlehem!'

The pilgrims hurried along the west bank of the Rhine. It was early in the morning, so that very few people would be scared when, in the course of a short second or two, they saw five sheep, two shepherds, two Kings of Orient, two angels of the Lord, and a little girl dressed in clothes very different from those that were usual in the Middle Ages.

When they tumbled into the town of Worms in the year of Our Lord 1162, they met a rider on horseback – a soldier who had been out on night duty, perhaps. The angel Impuriel flew over to the man, buzzed round him like a excited bumble bee, and repeated 'Fear not! Fear not! Fear not!'

The poor man was extremely scared. He spurred on his horse and galloped away round some low buildings. He didn't even have time to say 'Alleluia' or 'God be praised'.

'You only need to say it once,' Ephiriel chided Impuriel, 'but you must say it in a gentle, soft, heavenly voice. "Feear no-ot!" you must say. It's a good idea to keep your arms down too, to show you're not carrying a weapon.'

Balthazar the Wise Man pointed up at a cathedral with six towers.

'Everywhere and at all times people have stretched their

arms out to God,' he said. 'The church towers point up to heaven too, but they last much longer.'

The shepherds bent their heads respectfully at these wise words, and Elisabet felt she had to repeat them to herself before she was quite certain what he meant.

Joshua said, 'To Bethlehem! To Bethlehem!'

In the city of Basle on the southern bank of the Rhine they stopped in front of another big cathedral.

'The time tells us that 1119 years have passed since the Christ-child was born,' announced Ephiriel. 'This cathedral with five naves has just celebrated its centenary. But for hundreds of years Basle has been an important crossroads for travellers who have journeyed through the Alps between Italy and Northern Europe. We are going to follow the same route over the St Bernard Pass.'

'To Bethlehem!' said Joshua the shepherd, striking his crook on the ground. 'To Bethlehem!'

Whereupon they set off upwards through the Swiss mountains.

JOACHIM SAT IN bed, thinking about the strange pilgrimage to Bethlehem. After a while his mother and father came in to read what was on the piece of paper.

'We took home a small miracle from the bookshop, didn't we, Joachim?' said Papa. 'Can you imagine how it was made?'

'I think John made it,' said Joachim.

'The bookseller said something about someone called John, didn't he?'

Joachim wondered whether he ought to tell Mama and Papa that he had met John. But he didn't. He had to keep *one* little secret for himself. Because there was something else as well: SABET ... TEBAS ... SABET ... TEBAS.

'If this calendar was made by a flower-seller,' said Papa, 'he's certainly inventive.'

Mama agreed. 'Yes, he has plenty of imagination.'

'You said *I* had a lot of imagination when I told you about Elisabet and Ephiriel,' he said. 'But *I'd* only read all the scraps of paper in the Advent calendar.'

'And now we're saying that the person who made the Advent calendar has a lot of imagination,' said Mama. 'In a way it's the same.'

Joachim shook his head.

'He may not have so much imagination if the whole story is true.'

Papa laughed. 'You surely don't think you really can run all the way to Bethlehem and far back in time as well?'

'Nothing is impossible for God,' said Joachim.

Nobody protested. Papa thought they ought to get hold of a large atlas so that they could follow Elisabet's journey on the map. He had a historical atlas too, a book of maps that showed what all the countries and all the places were called in the olden days. The same country and the same town have often had many different names, he explained.

Suddenly Mama gave a little gasp.

'Do you remember that old story from way back?' she said to Papa. 'There really *was* a little girl who disappeared from this town while she and her mother were out doing their Christmas shopping. I think *she* was called Elisabet.'

Papa nodded. 'It was some time after the war. *Was* she called Elisabet?'

'I think so,' said Mama, 'but I'm not sure.'

Suddenly it was as if Mama and Papa had forgotten Joachim, they were so busy talking to each other.

'So maybe he's remembered that old story and made up the rest himself,' suggested Papa. 'If it *is* this flower-seller who's made it.'

'Can you find out whether she was called Elisabet?' said Joachim.

'Yes, I should think so,' replied Papa. 'Not that it really matters what she was called.'

The last person to say anything before they had to hurry to eat breakfast was Joachim.

'I think it matters a lot,' he said, 'because the lady in the photo was called Elisabet too.'

the
TWELFTH
OF DECEMBER

. . . for there's no sense in believing what's right unless

it leads to helping people in distress . . .

WHEN PAPA CAME home from work on the eleventh of December Mama and Joachim were waiting for him.

'Have you found out what she was called?' asked Joachim.

'Let me in first,' complained Papa. 'Yes, she was called Elisabet. Elisabet Hansen, in fact. It happened in December 1948.'

Dinner was ready, so they sat down at the table.

'I went into the bookshop as well,' continued Papa. 'I went into the storeroom with him, and there he found a photo that the flower-seller had once put in his window in exchange for a glass of water. I have it in my briefcase.'

'Then fetch it,' said Mama.

So he did. He put the picture on the table. Joachim snatched it and Mama leaned over it.

It showed a young woman with long fair hair. Round her neck she was wearing a silver cross set with a red stone. She was leaning against a small car. At the top of the photo was a large dome. At the bottom was written 'Elisabet'.

'Hm, no last name,' said Papa. 'It's not exactly an unusual name, but it's written in Norwegian. In many countries Elisabet is spelt differently.'

'Do you think she's not Norwegian, then?' asked Mama.

'No idea,' said Papa. 'But look at the photo carefully. The

dome in the background is St Peter's in Rome. She's standing in the road that leads to St Peter's Square. The car dates from the end of the fifties.'

'I feel almost scared,' whispered Mama. 'What are we getting mixed up in?'

'Yes, it's a mystery. But there's no reason to believe that the girl who disappeared in 1948 is the same as the woman in the photograph,' said Papa.

He sat staring in front of him. 'He wasn't at the market,' he said.

'Who? You're talking in riddles,' said Mama.

'The flower-seller, John, the man with the water. I'd give a lot for a talk with him. For there's one thing we *can* take for granted: it was he who made this strange calendar. Now he's disappeared.'

That was all he said. Joachim was thinking about it all so much that he wanted to go to bed early. Then it wouldn't be so long before it was morning again, and he'd get to know more about Elisabet Hansen and the angel Ephiriel.

When he woke up on the twelfth of December Mama and Papa were in his room before he had managed to open his eyes. That was a bit special because it was Saturday, when Joachim was usually up long before the others.

'*You* must open the calendar,' said Papa. 'Hurry up!'

It was obvious that he would have liked to open it himself.

The picture was of a man in a red tunic, holding a large sign.

Mama and Papa sat on the bed. Joachim had picked up a little piece of paper, folded over and over. He smoothed it out and read aloud what was written on the paper in very tiny writing.

QUIRINIUS

THE FIVE SHEEP had crossed a ridge and begun to run down into a fertile agricultural district. Impuriel fluttered round the little flock, and after the sheep and the cherub came Jacob and Joshua, Caspar and Balthazar, Ephiriel and Elisabet.

They passed Lake Biel and then several more lakes. The biggest and most beautiful was Lake Geneva. It glittered so that it looked as if a piece of heaven had fallen down to earth. Only when Elisabet looked up and saw that there was no hole in the sky was she able to be quite sure that the picture of the sky in the big lake was only a reflection.

Again they ran along an old road alongside a river in a deep valley. Ephiriel told them that the river was called the Rhône and that all the water it carried with it from the Alps ran down first into Lake Geneva, and later right down to the Mediterranean.

They ran across an old bridge to the other side of the river and stopped in front of a monastery called St Maurice. There were high Alps on every side with snow on their peaks.

'The time is 1079 after Christ,' said Ephiriel. 'The monks have lived here among these tall mountains, praising God and His creation, ever since the seventh century. The monastery is built around the grave of the holy St Maurice who was killed here in this valley in the year 285 because he refused to worship the Roman gods.'

He had only just finished speaking when a monk walked out of the monastery. He greeted them with a slight nod.

'Gloria Dei,' he said.

'And the same to you,' said Elisabet, even though she had

not understood what the monk was saying. She thought one of them ought to answer him.

Only then did the monk notice the two angels. He knelt on the grass and said, 'Alleluia! Alleluia!'

It was clear that they weren't used to angels visiting them at the monastery, even though it was so high up in the Alps that it was close to the angels in heaven.

Impuriel rose above the ground, flew towards the monk, gently beating his wings, and said in a voice soft as silk, 'Fear not, and be in no wise afraid. We are only going to Bethlehem to greet the Christ-child.'

Then King Caspar of Nubia strode up to the monk. He said, 'Peace be with you and your monastery. It is true what the angel has said. We are on our way to the Holy Land to pay homage to the King of Kings in Bethlehem, the city of David.'

With those words they set off again. They came to a little place called Martigny where there was an old Roman theatre.

'The Romans used this route over the Alps too,' explained the angel Ephiriel. 'Much later Napoleon crossed the Alps with his army.'

'To Bethlehem!' called Joshua, and they sped upwards towards the high mountains. The air was so thin and clear that Elisabet thought she must be on the way to heaven. From time to time they saw a mountain hare, a marmot or an Alpine goat. Up in the air circled crows and vultures, and now and again a grouse started up from the bushes.

At the top of the mountain pass stood a large house.

'The time is 1045 years after Christ,' said the angel Ephiriel. 'That house is a hospice whose purpose is to look after people who are crossing the Alps. It's brand new and has been built by Bernard of Menton. From now on and for the rest of time the Benedictine monks will live up here and organise a rescue service for people who are lost in the mountains. They are helped by their clever St Bernard dogs.'

'Right!' said the cherub Impuriel. 'For Jesus wanted to teach humans to help one another when they were in distress. Once he told a story about a man who was on his way from Jerusalem to Jericho, and was attacked by robbers who left him half dead at the side of the road. Several priests passed by, but none of them bent down to help the poor man, though he was in danger of losing his life. Jesus thought there wasn't much point in being priests if they couldn't even be bothered to help a fellow human being in distress. They might just as well forget all their prayers.'

Elisabet nodded, and Impuriel continued, 'But then a Samaritan came past, and Samaritans were not very popular in Judea, because their religion was a bit different from that of the Jews. But the Samaritan had compassion on him and helped the unfortunate man so that he saved his life. Yes indeed! For there's no sense in *believing* what's right unless it leads to helping people in distress.'

Elisabet nodded again and hid the cherub's words in her heart.

At one point where the pass forked a man was standing with a large sign in his hand. He was wearing a long red tunic. If he had not moved, one might have thought he was a petrified Roman from the Roman Empire.

On the sign was written 'TO BETHLEHEM' in capital letters. An arrow had been drawn in as well, to show which path they should follow.

'A living road sign!' exclaimed Elisabet.

Ephiriel nodded. 'Verily I say unto you, that road sign must be one of us.'

Impuriel was so excited that he flew right up to the man and shouted at him, 'Fear not! Fear not! Fear not!'

But the man with the sign was not at all affrighted. He took a step towards Elisabet, offered her his hand and said, 'Congrat— ... no, no, that wasn't quite correct. I mean, at your service, my friends! The very first thing I must remember to do is to say my name because I, too, have been allowed to take part in this Advent calendar. My name is Quirinius, Governor of Syria ... attractive appearance, closer acquaintance desired ... well, well, the most important thing is, of course, to be good and kind. Dixi!'

Elisabet couldn't help laughing; he talked so oddly. It was as if there were two people talking at once, for he interrupted himself the whole time. He handed her the sign. He had perhaps been standing and holding it for an eternity with the wind flapping in his tunic. He said, 'And this ... I am asking for your attention, my friends ... for here I have the actual prize ... I ought to say that this prize is for you. Dixi!'

'Am I to have the sign?' said Elisabet in astonishment.

And Quirinius replied, 'Only on the one side ... I mean you must turn it right round, you understand. Dixi!'

Elisabet didn't understand why he said Dixi all the time, for there was no dog or cat anywhere near. But the angel Ephiriel whispered that 'dixi' was Latin and meant that he had finished speaking.

Elisabet turned the sign round and saw to her great surprise that what she was holding in her hand was an Advent calendar with twenty-four doors to be opened. Above each door was painted a picture of a young woman with fair hair. She was standing in front of a church with a large dome on top.

'The first twelve,' said Quirinius. 'You may open the first

twelve doors, for we've come exactly so far on our journey. Dixi!'

Elisabet sat down on a rock and opened the first door. Behind it was a picture of a lamb. Behind the next door was an angel and behind the third a sheep. Then there followed pictures of a shepherd, another sheep, a King of Orient, a sheep, a shepherd, a sheep, a cherub, and another King of Orient. Elisabet saw that they were pictures of everyone who had joined the pilgrimage on its long way through Europe.

But who was the lady?

'Thank you very much!' she said.

Quirinius shook his head. 'On the contrary! What you said last was quite wrong, because *you're* not the one to say thank you ... I am. I thank you and others here for allowing an old Roman like myself to join this godly group which is on the right way to Bethlehem. After all, it was not I – in fact it was you – who set off first after the delightful lamb. Dixi! Dixi! Dixi!'

Elisabet looked up at Ephiriel and laughed.

'But you haven't opened the twelfth door,' said the angel.

Elisabet opened the twelfth door as well, and now she was looking down at a tiny picture of a fair-haired woman in front of the big dome of a church.

Joshua struck his shepherd's crook against a cairn.

'To Bethlehem! To Bethlehem!'

'How far is it to Bethlehem now?' asked Elisabet.

'Not very far!' said Ephiriel.

THEY SAT LOOKING at each other. Then Joachim began to laugh.

'I hope Quirinius is going all the way to Bethlehem with them,' he said.

Mama and Papa went on examining the piece of paper.

'He's brought the young woman into the story of little Elisabet today,' said Papa.

'And then, he's made another little Advent calendar inside the big one,' said Mama.

Papa nodded. 'Of course he must have meant something by it.'

'Do you think there's yet another calendar inside the little Advent calendar?' asked Joachim.

'Who knows?' said Mama. 'Who knows?'

the
THIRTEENTH
OF DECEMBER

... just as lightning sweeps across the sky,

pouring out a flood of light over the landscape

for a second or two ...

WHEN JOACHIM WOKE on the thirteenth of December his mother and father were in his room already. Joachim knew they were as curious as he was to see what was in the Advent calendar.

'*You* get to open it, my lad,' said Papa.

Joachim sat up and fished out the folded piece of paper. The picture in the calendar showed a rainbow.

He sat in bed with Mama on one side of him and Papa on the other. They both leaned over him while Mama read what was on the sheet of paper.

THE SIXTH SHEEP

A LITTLE PROCESSION was running down the steep mountains in the Alps from the St Bernard Pass. They spent only half a second in each place, for they were running, not just down the steep slopes towards Val d'Aosta in Northern Italy – they were speeding down through history too.

So a party of monks, who were on their way up from Val d'Aosta one day in June, in the year 998, saw them for only a short moment – just as lightning sweeps across the sky, pouring out a flood of light over the landscape for a second or two.

'Look!' exclaimed one of the monks.

'What?' asked the other.

'I thought I saw a strange procession on its way down through the valley. There were people and animals. Behind them all ran a little girl with an angel.'

The third monk agreed. 'I saw them too. It was like a heavenly host.'

The monk who had seen nothing shook his head in disbelief.

'Are you sure you can stand the thin air up here?' he asked.

He said that because he had looked down at an azalea at the instant when the pilgrimage had passed.

Four years earlier a party of merchants from Milan had seen the same as the two monks. That had been a few kilometres further down the valley.

The godly throng stopped for a little while to enjoy the view over the beautiful Val d'Aosta. Ephiriel pointed up at Mont Blanc and the sharp peak of the Matterhorn. Elisabet was more interested in studying the Advent calendar she had been given by the Governor of Syria.

She pointed at opening number 12 where there was a picture of an Advent calendar exactly the same as the one she had in her hand, turned to Quirinius and asked, 'Can I open the doors in the tiny little calendar as well?'

Quirinius shook his head. 'Unfortunately not. That calendar is sealed with seven seals. Dixi!'

'We are such Wise Men that we can reveal what is inside it, all the same,' said Caspar the first Wise Man. 'Something mysterious is written there in tiny little letters.'

'Tell me, then!' said Elisabet.

'Behind the first door is written Elisabet,' Caspar began. 'Behind the second is written Lisabet, and behind the third Isabet. Then come Sabet, Abet, Bet and Et. That's the first seven doors.'

'And what then?' said Elisabet, with a broad smile.

Balthazar, the second Wise Man, replied, 'After that come Te, Teb, Teba, Tebas, Tebasi, Tebasil and Tebasile. Then there are only ten doors left.'

'What's behind them?'

'Elisabet, Lisabet, Isabet, Sabet, Abet, Bet and Et.'

'But then there are still three doors left,' said Elisabet.

Caspar nodded solemnly. 'Behind door number 22 is written Roma, behind door number 23 is written Amor, and behind door number 24 the name Jesus is written in very beautiful and artistic lettering. One letter is red, the second is orange, the third is yellow, the fourth blue, and the fifth violet. Altogether that makes all the colours of the rainbow. Jesus was like a whole rainbow.'

'Why?'

'When it's been raining heavily, and the sun breaks through the dark clouds, the rainbow appears in the sky. It's as if a little bit of Jesus is in the air, for Jesus was a rainbow between heaven and earth.'

Joshua lifted up his shepherd's crook and struck a stone with such force that it echoed all round the mountains.

'To Bethlehem!' he said. 'To Bethlehem!'

And it was as if the mountains replied, 'Lehem, Lehem, Lehem...'

It didn't take long for them to reach the Valley of the Po. That is the name of the fertile country that lies around the great River Po, which flows from the Italian Alps in the west to the Adriatic Sea in the east. Ephiriel told them they would be going the same way as the river.

They travelled through the countryside until the River Po met another big river called the Ticino, near the trading city of Pavia. Ephiriel told them that the angel watch showed 904 and that Pavia already had a university that was famous throughout Europe.

Joshua was about to strike the ground with his shepherd's crook in order to say something Elisabet was about to say, but Jacob the shepherd spoke first. He pointed down at a large raft that was lying by the river bank and said, 'We'll borrow that.'

So the whole of the long procession of pilgrims jumped on board the raft.

As they were about to push off from the bank, a man came running towards them with a sheep in his arms.

'Accept my sincere offering!' he said.

So six sheep had to be crammed together on the narrow raft.

When they were out on the river, Quirinius said that Elisabet could open door number 13 in the advent calendar. Behind it was a picture of a man carrying a sheep.

WHEN MAMA HAD finished reading, the family sat on the bed for a long time without saying anything.

'Lehem, Lehem, Lehem!' said Mama at last, almost as if she were singing it.

'Sabet ... Tebas,' said Joachim.

He surprised himself. There it was again! John had in fact mumbled half Elisabet's name. And he'd never thought of it before! Then he had said the same half of her name backwards.

But why had he done that?

Papa had something to say too.

'If only I could find this flower-seller maybe we'd find the answer to how the Advent calendar was made. Or *why*, as far as that goes. I'm curious to find out what makes a grown man sit clipping and glueing and playing with letters in this way.'

'I'm sure it's in order to spread some of the glory of heaven,' observed Joachim. 'I believe the magic Advent calendar is a small part of the glory of heaven that has strayed down to earth. Up there it's so full of wonderful things that they can easily be scattered.'

Mama and Papa couldn't help laughing. It was only after they had read through all the folded sheets of paper that they had understood why Joachim had said so many strange things recently.

'I'm thinking about the three monks in Val d'Aosta,' said Mama.

Papa and Joachim looked at her. Then she said, 'We're sitting here almost like those monks. We have something on our hands and we don't quite know whether we can believe it.'

Joachim could no longer manage to keep his meeting with John secret. It was as if this last little secret was exploding inside his head, so it was good to let it out.

'John was at the gate one day when I came home from school,' he said. 'He got our address from the man in the bookshop.'

'And you didn't tell us?' said Papa.

'I didn't think it was important. He only wanted to know who I was.'

'Yes, yes. But what did he *tell* you?' said Papa impatiently. 'He must have said something about the magic Advent calendar?'

'He said it wasn't Christmas yet. Then he said he'd tell me more about Elisabet another time.'

Papa nodded. 'I'll drop by the market again today. I intend to meet this John, even if I have to lasso him.'

But when he got home again, he could only throw up his arms.

'Gone!' he said. 'As if the earth had swallowed him up.'

All that afternoon Joachim repeated two names inside himself: Elisabet ... Tebasile ... Elisabet.

One name was like a reflection of the other. But when Joachim looked at himself in the mirror, he saw himself, even though the picture in the mirror was reversed.

Could it all be a secret message that the two Elisabets were one and the same person? But Tebasile sounded like a proper name too.

Could there be someone called Tebasile as well?

That evening Joachim lay for a long time staring at the ceiling before he could relax. In the end he had to get up and write something in his little notebook. It was something he had seen inside his head.

He wrote:

```
S A B E T
A         E
B         B
E         A
T E B A S
```

the
FOURTEENTH
OF DECEMBER

... even before the child's forefinger

had time to unfold ...

T HE NEXT DAY Joachim woke up before Mama and
Papa. He sat up in bed. Only ten days left till Christmas Eve.

What was going to happen to Elisabet, the angel Ephiriel,
and all the others who were going to Bethlehem?

Before he managed to open the Advent calendar, Mama
and Papa were in his room.

'Let's get going,' said Papa. Under his arm he had two large
atlases.

Joachim opened the door with the number 14 on it. The
folded piece of paper fell down into the bed, and they saw a
picture of a raft with people, animals and angels on it.

They sat on the edge of the bed. That day it was Joachim's
turn to read.

ISAAC

T OWARDS THE END of the ninth century a strange raft
was sailing on the River Po in the direction of the
Adriatic Sea to the east. The country they were sailing
through was called Lombardy. On the raft stood a small flock
of sheep, bleating crossly because they were not allowed to
drink the river water. The smallest sheep was scuttling to

and fro, so that a little bell hanging round its woolly neck was tinkling.

Two Wise Men were pointing at objects around them, and saying wise words about the beautiful country they were sailing through. After a long discussion about the blessings of oranges and dates, they agreed that God could not have created a better world – at least, not in six days.

At the back of the raft stood a man in Roman clothes, steering with a long oar. Such clothes had not been long out of fashion. He was talking to a small girl who was holding a piece of cardboard in her hands. On one side was written, 'TO BETHLEHEM'; on the other was a picture of a young woman with long fair hair.

Most conspicuous were two angels standing forwards on the raft, beating their wings to stop the boat drifting towards the river bank. This was long before river boats were equipped with propellers.

Now and again the cherub Impuriel turned to the others and praised the beauty of the landscape they were sailing through.

'Wonderful!' he called out. 'Nothing but glory and joy. It's just like on the fifth day when God saw everything that He had made. And behold – it was very good!'

Once or twice somebody on the shore noticed them. But the raft was revealed for only a brief second. That's because it wasn't just sailing down the Valley of the Po, it was sailing down through history too, crossing the tidal wave of the age. When a little child stood on the bank of the river and pointed at the strange raft, it disappeared even before the child's forefinger had time to unfold.

So perhaps it was only a reflection?

They passed old Roman bridges and buildings, theatres,

temples and aqueducts. The angel Ephiriel pointed out all the churches.

'I was often in this area as a young man,' Quirinius told them, as he stared down at the long oar in the water. 'But that was a very long time ago . . . or the opposite, of course. I mean, it's still a good while before we get there. Dixi!'

Elisabet realised that he was talking about the Roman period when there were Roman soldiers nearly everywhere in the world.

'What did it look like here then?' she asked.

'The Roman theatres are still standing. The orange trees as well – and the red poppies along the river bank. But nobody had heard about Jesus. What's new are all the churches and monasteries, priests and monks. Dixi! Dixi!'

Before long Joshua pointed at the river bank. 'We'll land over there.'

Quirinius tried to steer the raft towards land, and was helped by the two angels who beat their wings energetically. While Joshua the shepherd drew the raft up to a tree with his crook, the angel Ephiriel said a few warning words to the cherub imp.

'If we meet any people you must be sure to remember to say "Fear not" in a gentle angel voice, so that they will not be afraid. We're only visiting, so it's important that we behave properly.'

All the pilgrims alighted from the raft, those on two legs, those on four, and those with wings on their shoulders. They passed a country church and turned uphill through the countryside.

The towns were not very large at this period, but soon they were approaching one of the largest. Ephiriel told them it was called Padua.

Just before they sped through the town gate they caught sight of a man in a blue tunic. He was sitting on a stone with his head in his hands. It looked as if he had been sitting there for a very long time.

Impuriel flew towards him, hovered in the air right in front of him, fluttering his wings, and said, 'Fear not and be in no wise afraid. I am Impuriel and am one of God's angels who is out on a sacred errand.'

It looked as if the cherub's words had an effect, for the man did not throw himself to the ground and did not hide his head. He said neither 'Alleluia' nor 'Gloria Dei'. He simply got to his feet and walked towards them.

'Then he is one of us,' said Ephiriel.

The man offered his hand to Elisabet.

'I am Isaac the shepherd and I am going the same way as you.'

That made it much easier to guide the six sheep through Padua.

Altogether there were fifteen of them, going at such a speed that the few people who were out in the streets didn't have time to look at them before they vanished. The pilgrims only just managed to see the inhabitants of the town, too. When they glimpsed an early riser, the man or woman disappeared in the next instant, perhaps to be replaced by a different man or woman.

Elisabet thought they were in the town for only half a minute, but in fact the strange pilgrimage haunted the streets of Padua for seven or eight long years; for that half-minute consisted of thirty brief seconds, and those thirty brief seconds were divided between all those seven or eight years.

Ancient accounts tell us that there was never so much talk of angels in Padua as during those magic years from 804 to

811. Now and then someone or other thought they had seen something strange in the streets. Could it have been a procession of angels who had swept through the town?

Outside the town walls they stopped in front of a small monastery.

'Strange to see a Roman town again,' said Quirinius. 'I wonder who's the emperor now.'

Ephiriel looked at his angel watch.

'It's exactly 800 years after Christ. On Christmas Day this year Charles the Great will be crowned Emperor of Rome.'

'Then we'll soon be starting on a new century,' said Joshua. He struck his shepherd's crook against the monastery wall.

'To Bethlehem! To Bethlehem!'

PAPA OPENED THE atlas, pointed out the River Po, and found the town of Padua. Then he turned the pages backwards and forwards and tried to trace with his finger the long distance the pilgrims had run.

'Here's Halden,' he began. 'Then they came down to the big lake in Sweden ... that must be Vänern. From there they hurried south through Sweden to Kungälv, Gothenburg, Halmstad and Lund. They rowed across to Sjaelland and visited Copenhagen. Yes, I can find it all. They arrived in Fyn and sprang through Odense. They were ferried across the strip of water called Little Belt to Jutland. There they passed the towns of Kolding and Flensburg...'

'They travelled backwards in history as well,' said Mama.

But Papa merely went on following the path they had run, with his finger on the map.

'Here's Hamburg. Then Elisabet was left lying in the market in Hanover ... yes, here. And here's Hamelin, the town that had broken its solemn promise to the rat-catcher.'

'You broke a solemn promise too,' interrupted Joachim. 'You opened my secret box.'

Papa continued, 'Further south is Paderborn; this is where the cherub Impuriel flew down in spirals from the church tower. From there they ran to Cologne and continued up the Valley of the Rhine. And the angel Impuriel was quite right: it's wonderfully beautiful there.'

'That was during the thirteenth century,' said Mama.

'Wait a bit,' said Papa. 'I want to follow the whole route. In Mainz they met Balthazar, then it was Worms and Basle. Today Basle is in Switzerland.'

'But Elisabet was there in the twelfth century,' said Mama.

Papa went on searching with his finger.

'Here's Lake Biel and Lake Geneva. I've found the little place called Martigny ... this is a good map. Through the St Bernard Pass, yes ... today there are tunnels all over the place. Down through Val d'Aosta to Lombardy and the Valley of the Po.'

'Bravo!' said Mama. 'But they're travelling down through history as well. I think *that* journey is an even stranger one to think about.'

'But that's only something he's invented,' said Papa, looking up from his map.

'I think it's quite true,' said Joachim.

'Yes, who knows?' said Mama.

Papa only shook his head. 'Now I wonder which route they're going to take ...'

'Goodness, it's eight o'clock!' exclaimed Mama.

There was a bit of squabbling because they were so short

of time. Joachim thought there was nothing worse.

As he ran to school many strange names were buzzing in his head. Now he had seen all those places on the map.

At school they had started to rehearse a nativity play; Joachim's class would be putting it on in the gym on the last school day before Christmas. Joachim was going to be the Second Shepherd.

the
FIFTEENTH
OF DECEMBER

... 'Fear not,' he said, in a voice as soft as silk ...

WHEN JOACHIM WOKE up on the fifteenth of December there were only ten doors left to open in the magic Advent calendar. He didn't even have time to sit up in bed before Mama and Papa were in his room.

Joachim was no longer cross because they had opened his secret box. They had done something they had no right to, but he had forgiven them. He couldn't have gone on sulking about it for ever. Besides, it was more fun to read about Elisabet and the pilgrimage when Mama and Papa were sharing it. It was almost like having a birthday every day until Christmas Eve.

'Let's get going,' said Papa.

Joachim pulled himself up in bed and opened door number 15. He had to fish out the scrap of folded paper and be careful so that it didn't tear. The picture showed islands and skerries with houses on them; the small islands were bathed in radiant sunshine.

That day it was Papa's turn to read. He grabbed the piece of paper, cleared his throat twice, and read loudly and clearly from the fragile sheet.

THE SEVENTH SHEEP

THE PILGRIMS CAME to the Venetian lagoon at the top of the Adriatic Sea.

They paused on a little rise with a view over the lagoon, and Ephiriel started to point out all the islands and skerries that studded the water. On many of the islets the Venetians had built houses, on some of them churches as well. Several of the islets were so close together that bridges had been built between them. Everywhere there were scores of small fishing boats.

'The time is 797 years after Christ,' announced Ephiriel. 'We see the young Venice, which will soon be the name of the 118 islands. The Venetians settled here in order to be protected from the sea pirates and barbarians who were roving about. Exactly a hundred years ago they all combined under a leader called the Doge.'

'I can't see any gondolas,' complained Elisabet. 'I thought there would be more bridges too.'

Ephiriel laughed. 'But you're not in the Venice of the twentieth century. I said the time was 797, and that people had lived here for only a couple of centuries. But Venice will soon become so thickly populated that one island will scarcely be separated from another.'

While they stood looking out over all the small islets and islands, a rowing boat came past. One end was filled with salt. In the other end stood some sheep, bleating at the sun which was about to break through the morning mist.

The man who was rowing the boat was so frightened when he caught sight of the procession of pilgrims that he covered his eyes with his arm, took a step backwards, and lost his balance so that he fell head over heels into the water. Elisabet saw him come to the surface a few seconds later and then go under again.

'He's drowning!' she cried. 'We must save him.'

But the angel Ephiriel was already on his way. He hovered gracefully above the glittering water, seized the man when he surfaced again and lifted him up on land, dripping wet. Ephiriel drew in the rowing boat.

The man lay down on the ground and coughed fit to burst his lungs. He gasped for breath and said, 'Gratie, gratie . . .'

Elisabet tried to explain that they were on their way to Bethlehem to greet the Christ-child and that he needn't be frightened. Impuriel had begun circling round him.

'Fear not,' he said, in a voice as soft as silk, 'and be in no wise afraid. But you should not have been all alone on the sea if you can't swim, for you can't always expect an angel to be around. We wander about only *very* rarely, you know.'

It didn't look as if Impuriel's advice was any comfort to the man, but the cherub sat down beside him, patted him on the cheek, and went on repeating 'Fear not'. It must have had an effect, for the man got to his feet and trudged back to his boat. He lifted a little lamb out of it and walked back towards them.

'Agnus Dei,' he said.

That means 'God's Lamb', and the lamb joined the rest of the flock of sheep without protest. Joshua struck his shepherd's crook on the ground and said, 'To Bethlehem! To Bethlehem!' and they sprang off again.

At the very end of the Venetian Gulf stood the old Roman town of Aquileia. As they ran, Ephiriel pointed to a monastery.

'The time is 718 years after Christ. But there have been Christian communities here from ancient times.'

The procession of pilgrims sped on through the town of Trieste. Then they continued south, across country, through Croatia.

PAPA PUT THE scrap of paper down on the bed and opened one of the large atlases that he had placed on Joachim's desk.

'Here's Venice,' he said, 'and here's Trieste; that's on the border of Jugoslavia. I can't find Aquileia.'

'But maybe it doesn't exist any more,' said Mama. 'You must look in the historical atlas as well.'

Papa fetched the other atlas. There were maps of all the countries in Europe, but the names of the countries and the towns were different from one map to the other.

'Find a map of the area for the eighth century,' said Mama.

Papa turned the pages of the atlas over and over. 'Here it is! Aquileia! The old town was situated halfway between Venice and Trieste. This is quite fantastic...'

'What is?' asked Joachim.

'John must have used old maps like this too, for the world changes the whole time. History is like a big pile of pancakes where each pancake is a new map of the world.'

'Pancakes?' said Joachim.

Papa nodded. 'It's never enough to ask *where* something's happening and it's not enough to ask *when* something's happening. You always have to ask both when and where.'

He put both hands on top of Joachim's hands.

'Imagine that you have twenty pancakes piled on top of each other. If there's a black speck on one of the pancakes, and you have to find that particular speck, you must find out which of the twenty pancakes the black speck is on, and exactly where on the pancake. You may have to leaf through the whole pile.'

Joachim nodded, and Papa went on, 'The long journey to Bethlehem is all about a journey that goes right through all twenty pancakes. Elisabet doesn't just travel around on the top pancake. She's moving through the whole mountain of them.'

Now Joachim understood what Papa meant.

'They're travelling down through twenty centuries,' said Papa. 'There are maps in this book that show how the world looked in every one of the twenty centuries. I think John must have been reading a pancake book like this.'

Papa and Joachim couldn't help laughing when Papa said 'pancake book'.

'The big question is whether there really *was* a man who was saved by an angel in Venice in the year 797. Do you believe it's possible to find out?' said Mama.

'Surely you don't think all this story is *true*?' said Papa.

'No, I suppose not,' said Mama, wavering. 'But if it really *had* happened, the man would be bound to have talked about it, to the priest for instance. Then it might have been written about in books. Maybe we ought to search in the library shelves.'

Papa didn't want to hear any more. Instead he said, 'Let's go and have a pizza in town and go to the market afterwards. You remember what he looks like, Joachim?'

'Of course,' said Joachim. 'I'd know him at once. He talked a bit oddly, but then, he may not be Norwegian.'

That day Mama met Joachim at school, and they took the

bus to town to meet Papa. From the pizza restaurant they could look down on the market in front of the cathedral.

As they ate Papa kept asking, 'Can you see him, Joachim?' and every time Joachim had to answer no. John wasn't at the market selling flowers any more.

They bought some chunky candles and a couple of Christmas presents, then went into the bookshop where Joachim had found the magic Advent calendar.

The bookseller recognised Papa and Joachim at once, and shook Mama's hand too.

'Here we are again,' said Papa. 'We wondered whether you had seen anything of this remarkable flower-seller.'

The bookseller shook his head. 'It's quite a while since he was here. He's not usually around much at this time of year.'

'The magic Advent calendar is a bit of a mystery,' explained Mama. 'We wanted to invite him home to us, to thank him for it properly.'

They agreed that the bookseller should ask John to phone them.

'Just one more thing,' said Papa as they were leaving. 'Do you know what country he comes from?'

'I think he said he was born in Damascus,' said the bookseller.

When they were in the car going home, Papa sat drumming his fingers on the steering wheel. 'If only we had found that man!' he said.

'At least we found out where he comes from,' replied Mama. 'Isn't Damascus the capital of Syria?'

the
SIXTEENTH
OF DECEMBER

... every person's imagination is a little different ...

FOR THE REST of the evening they talked about Elisabet, John, and the magic Advent calendar. Even when nobody said anything, they all knew what the others were thinking about.

Papa might drop a fork on the floor while he was clearing the dinner table and say, 'Pity we can't find him. But I expect he's a cunning fellow, and cunning fellows are very difficult to catch.'

Mama might be sitting with the newspaper on her lap, staring in front of her, when she said, 'After all, it's a mystery all on its own why the poor little girl never came back.'

Joachim had put the photo of the grown-up Elisabet on the mantelpiece. He would suddenly look up from the television to the old photograph and say, 'Maybe she was his girlfriend.'

Mama and Papa heard what he said. Papa put a cup on the coffee table. 'Yes, maybe.'

'Because inside that tiny little Advent calendar,' continued Mama, 'the one inside the Advent calendar that Quirinius gave Elisabet, was written, not just Elisabet and Tebasile. There was Roma and Amor as well. Amor means love.'

'But that's Roma backwards,' said Joachim. 'So perhaps Tebasile really means something as well.'

Early on the morning of the sixteenth of December Mama

and Papa came in to Joachim and woke him up.

'Wake up, Joachim,' said Mama. 'It's only seven o'clock, but we need some extra time together these days.'

Joachim rubbed sleep out of his eyes and looked up at all the doors in the Advent calendar. He thought again that the magic Advent calendar was like having a birthday every day. Would it be possible to make a calendar like that to last the whole year, he wondered?

He remembered something he had dreamed. A little girl had crawled down through a whole load of pancakes to look for something she had lost. In the end she found it on the pancake at the very bottom. It was a tiny doll, wrapped in a piece of cloth. But in the dream the doll was alive.

'Come on, open it, then!' said Papa, almost crossly. 'We must get going.'

Joachim sat up and found the door with the number 16 on it. The folded sheet of paper fell out on to the bed, but Papa picked it up quickly. Behind the door was a picture of an old castle.

'I'll read it,' said Mama. It was her turn that day.

They made themselves comfortable.

DANIEL

I T HAPPENED IN the days when the old Roman Empire was divided into two. In both East and West the Christian religion had taken root in the people, but the Christian world was still being plundered by heathen peoples. They delayed the building of new churches, stole gold and silver, and pillaged whole cities.

A decree was sent out from the Pope in Rome that the

Church's property should be defended against the foreign races who had not yet heard about Jesus. That was when a strange procession advanced through time and space on its way to Bethlehem, the city of David. They came from a distant future.

At Salonae in Dalmatia they stopped in front of the ancient ruins of a Roman imperial palace. At first the ruins seemed abandoned, but the godly company entered by way of a small gate in the wall and discovered that they were teeming with people. It was like tearing the bark away from an old log to see insects creeping inside.

When the angel Ephiriel saw all the people in the town he said, 'The angel watch says 688 years after Christ. We are standing inside the walls of the palace of the Emperor Diocletian. Diocletian was born in this part of the country about 250 years after Christ. He fought against the nomadic tribes and tried to rebuild the old Roman Empire. He closed the Christian churches and started to persecute the Christians cruelly. When he died he was buried here in the great palace. But only a few years after his death the whole of the Roman Empire became Christian. A complete town grew up inside the old palace. Much later this town will be called Split.'

While Ephiriel was talking a half-naked little boy caught sight of them and called out, 'Angelos! Angelos!'

'What does that mean?' Elisabet asked Ephiriel.

'It means angels. I don't suppose he's met very many of us before.'

The next moment all the people had seen them. The children stood still and gazed up at them in amazement, but the grown-ups threw themselves down and murmured words like 'Gloria', 'Amen' and 'Alleluia' over and over again.

Impuriel began hovering above their heads.

'Be not in the slightest bit afraid,' he said. 'For 688 years ago there was born unto you in Bethlehem, the city of David, the best ever saviour. Now we are travelling from the four corners of the earth to pay Him homage.'

A man in black clothes came towards them.

'The priest,' whispered Ephiriel.

He said something that Elisabet didn't understand, but the angel explained that he was asking them to greet the Christ-child from this little corner too.

Joshua struck his shepherd's crook against the old town wall and said, 'To Bethlehem! To Bethlehem!'

They hurried on down through Dalmatia. They sprang over hills and ridges and often had good views of the Adriatic Sea. Ephiriel pointed to a small harbour town below.

'The time is 659. That little town is called Ragusa and has just been founded by Greeks from Peloponnesus. Later on the town will become an important trading and shipping centre and will be called Dubrovnik.'

On a rise with a view over the sea they met another shepherd, who was sitting under a pine tree to protect himself from the strong sun. He had the same light blue tunic as Joshua, Jacob and Isaac. When he saw the procession of pilgrims approaching, he got to his feet and came to meet them.

'Glory to God in the highest,' he said. 'My name is Daniel and I have been waiting here for many years, but I knew you would pass through Dalmatia some time during the seventh century. I am coming with you to Bethlehem.'

'Yes, indeed!' said Impuriel the cherub. 'For you are one of us.'

Joshua struck his crook against the pine tree.

'To Bethlehem! To Bethlehem!'

Soon they came to a large lake. At the end of the lake was a town.

'This town is called Scodra, and the lake is the Lake of Scodra,' said Ephiriel. 'After many centuries this land will be called Albania. We have left the Roman Catholic area now, and have reached the territory that will be governed from Byzantium.'

Elisabet was confused by all the strange names but the angel explained, 'The angel watch shows that 602 years have passed since Jesus was born. At this time, and throughout the Middle Ages, the Christian Church had two different capitals. The one is Rome, and the other is Byzantium at the entrance to the Black Sea.'

'But didn't they believe the same things?'

'On the whole, yes, but they showed it in slightly different ways. People have come and gone, and church traditions and services have come and gone too, even though the start of it all was something that happened one Christmas night in Bethlehem, the city of David.'

Impuriel ruffled his wings and said, 'Yes, indeed! For there was only one Mary and only one Christ-child. Since then many millions of images of Mary and the Christ-child have been painted and fashioned, and none of them are alike. For even though there was only one Christ-child, every person's imagination is a little different.'

Elisabet hid these words in her heart. But Impuriel beat his wings and came right up to her.

'God created only one Adam and one Eve as well. They were little children who played hide-and-seek and climbed the trees in the Garden of Eden, for there was no point in creating a lovely garden if there were no children who could play in it.

'But these two children ate the fruit of the Tree of Knowledge, and then they grew up. That was the end of playing in the world, but only for a short while, for soon grown-up Adam and grown-up Eve had children, and then grandchildren as well. So God saw to it that there would always be plenty of children in the world. There's no point in creating a whole world if there are no children to keep on discovering it. That's how God goes on creating the world over and over again. He will never quite finish it, for new children keep on arriving, and they discover the world for the very first time. Yes indeed!'

The two Wise Men looked at one another.

'Well, well!' said Balthazar.

'This explanation is perhaps a little dubious,' added Caspar. 'But all good stories may be understood in at least two or three ways, and only one story can be told at a time.'

'But even though many billions of children have lived on earth, no two of them have been exactly alike,' said Impuriel. 'There are no two blades of grass in the whole of creation that are exactly alike. That's because God in heaven is so full of imagination that every now and again it bubbles over and a little spills over on to the earth. "Fill the waters in the seas, and let fowl multiply in the earth," He said as He slaved away at creating the world in six days. "Let the earth bring forth the living creature after his kind, cattle, and creeping thing, and beast of the earth after his kind..."'

Impuriel peered sideways at Elisabet. 'I know it all by heart.'

Elisabet clapped her hands in admiration. She had always found it difficult to learn old stories and rhymes by heart.

Joshua thumped his shepherd's crook on the ground. 'To

Bethlehem! To Bethlehem!' On they went, up through the Macedonian highlands.

WHEN MAMA HAD finished reading they sat and smiled at one another.

'This flower-man certainly doesn't lack imagination,' said Papa.

He turned the pages of one of the atlases again. 'They've run through the whole of Jugoslavia. That's quite a lot for one day.'

'For a hundred years, you mean,' said Joachim. 'Every single day is a hundred years.'

'But that's only for us,' argued Mama. 'For Elisabet and all the others it goes very fast. Besides, it's not called Jugoslavia any more. It wasn't in the seventh century either. Then it was called Croatia and Dalmatia.'

Papa went on studying the map. He showed Joachim where they had been running. Finally he pointed out the towns of Split and Dubrovnik.

When Papa came home from work that afternoon he said, 'I went to the police today.'

'To find John?' said Mama.

Papa shook his head. 'No, no. I wanted to find out a bit more about this girl who disappeared in 1948. She was only seven years old and she really did vanish. The police searched for her for months, but she was never found. The only thing they did find was her knitted hat lying in some woodland just outside the town. So that child must have had a short life.'

'I don't think you can be certain of that,' said Mama.

Papa continued, 'I contacted her family too. I made a few phone calls, and finally managed to talk to her mother. She's now an old lady of over seventy.'

Mama and Joachim both spoke at once.

'What did she say?'

'Did she know John?'

'One question at a time, if you please,' said Papa. 'The old lady couldn't tell me much more than the police, but she *did* say that once, many, many years ago, she had talked to a man called John who came from Syria. The girl's father died a few years ago. He had travelled to Syria and many other countries. But she hadn't heard about the picture that was taken in Rome ten to fifteen years after Elisabet disappeared. I promised to send her a copy.'

After Mama and Papa had said goodnight, Joachim got out of bed again and sat at his desk.

Who was the young woman whom John had taken a picture of in Rome? Was she called Elisabet – or something quite different?

'Sabet ... Tebas ...' he had said. But why had he said that? They sounded almost like sorcerers' words.

Joachim opened his notebook and looked at the way he had written the two names before. Now he wrote:

```
S A B E T E B A S
A         E         A
B         B         B
E         A         E
T E B A S A B E T
E         A         E
B         B         B
A         E         A
S A B E T E B A S
```

Was that a window? Or was it a cross?

Perhaps it was supposed to be an Advent calendar.

the
SEVENTEENTH
OF DECEMBER

... many things have been done in the name of Jesus

that heaven is not very happy about ...

ON THE SEVENTEENTH of December Joachim woke first. He opened the Advent calendar to find a picture of the whole of the long procession of pilgrims on their way down a steep mountainside.

As soon as he had unfolded the little piece of paper, Papa came in. 'You haven't opened it already, have you?' he said. 'You might have waited for us.'

He hurried into the bedroom and hauled Mama out of bed. She wasn't even allowed to go to the bathroom first. Then they sat down on the edge of the bed and bent over the piece of paper. It was Papa's turn to read.

SERAPHIEL

IT WAS THE very end of the sixth century. Across the Macedonian chain of mountains sped a long procession of pilgrims.

Down on the bank of the River Axios a sheep farmer raised his eyes to the mountains and saw the seven sheep rolling down the mountainside like a pearl necklace. Around them fluttered a white bird. Behind the sheep came four men, one of them holding a shepherd's crook. Behind the four shepherds came even more people.

The amazing sight lasted only for a second or two, then it was gone. The Greek sheep farmer stood rubbing his eyes, but then he remembered that his father had told him once of a similar vision many years ago, when he saw a mysterious company escorted by two angels.

Long after the vision of the pilgrims' procession had gone, the sheep farmer realised that the white bird had not been a bird after all. He, too, had seen one of the angels of the Lord.

The pilgrims followed the river down to where it ran out into the Thermaic Gulf in the Aegean Sea. Elisabet had never seen such blue water.

Ephiriel pointed up at a mountain peak far away to the right of the Gulf they were gazing at.

'That's the peak of Mount Olympus. In the old days the Greeks believed the gods lived there. They were called Zeus and Apollo, Athene and Aphrodite. But now angel time tells us that 569 years have passed since the birth of Jesus, and there is no one who believes in the Greek gods any more.'

'Do they believe in Jesus?' asked Elisabet.

The angel nodded. 'But it's only a few years since the Church closed the ancient School of Philosophy in Athens. That was founded almost a thousand years ago by a famous philosopher called Plato.'

'Why did they have to close the old school?'

Ephiriel said something that Elisabet hid in her heart.

'Many things have been done in the name of Jesus that heaven is not very happy about. Jesus wanted to talk to everyone. He never asked them to keep silent. Only a few years later Paul came to Athens. He was the first great missionary for Christendom, and when he arrived in Athens he wanted to talk to the Greek philosophers. He asked them to listen to the words of the Lord, but he wanted to hear what they thought as well.'

He couldn't say any more because Joshua struck the ground with his shepherd's crook and said, 'To Bethlehem! To Bethlehem!'

After a while they came to a city which stood at the innermost point of the Gulf. Ephiriel said that the time was 551, that the city was called Thessalonica and that the Romans had made it the capital of Macedonia.

'As early as fifty years after the birth of Jesus Paul established a Christian community here. And we're still a long way from the Holy Land. Paul wrote two letters to the Christians in this city. We can read them to this day, for both those letters are in the Bible.'

Elisabet thought about the angel's words. She would not have believed it possible to keep a few letters so long.

They entered the city by the town gate. It was early in the morning and hardly a soul was to be seen in the streets. Ephiriel pointed to the many churches and said that some of them were already several hundred years old. He stopped beside one of them and said, 'Fifteen hundred years will pass, and this church of St George will still be standing here.'

Then they sped further east to another city.

'This is Philippi,' said Ephiriel. 'Here Paul made his first speech on European soil, and established the first Christian community in Europe. In the Bible there is a letter he wrote to the Philippians when he was imprisoned for the sake of his faith.'

Ephiriel pointed to an octagonal church. All of a sudden one of the doors was opened from the inside. Impuriel had already started to say, 'Fear not,' when a new angel strode out of the octagonal church. He took a few steps towards

Elisabet and said, 'Greetings, my daughter. I am Seraphiel, and I am coming with you to Bethlehem in order to ride on the clouds of heaven and welcome the Christ-child into the world.'

Joshua struck his shepherd's crook against the church wall.

'To Bethlehem! To Bethlehem!'

They set off along the old road between the Ionian Sea and Constantinople. Seraphiel told them that the road was called the Via Egnatia. As they ran, the angel Ephiriel said, 'The time is 511 years after Christ, and we shall be in Constantinople before it's 500.'

PAPA LEAFED THROUGH the atlas to see which way the pilgrims had gone.

'Here's the Macedonian mountain chain. Then they came down to the River Axios, that's here. And this is the Thermaic Gulf. When they're standing here they can see Mount Olympus on their right. That's correct. Yes, it all tallies.'

He opened the second atlas, the one that showed how the countries of Europe had looked in the sixth century.

'The Via Egnatia must be this road,' he said. 'Here you see Thessalonica and Philippi.'

'Isn't there a map of Paul's missionary journeys?' Mama wanted to know.

Papa turned the pages in the atlas over and over again. Joachim thought the way it showed how the world had looked in every age was like magic. It even showed cities that had long ago been buried in earth and sand.

'Here it is!' exclaimed Papa. He had found the map that showed Paul's four great missionary journeys. 'Paul visited Philippi and Thessalonica on his second missionary journey.'

When Joachim came home from school, the telephone was ringing. He thought it was Mama or Papa, for they sometimes rang to tell him they would be coming home a little later, or to say he could find something to eat in the refrigerator. He hated that.

He lifted the receiver. 'Hallo?'

'It's John,' came the answer.

'Where *have* you been?' he asked. That was what Mama said when he had been out with a friend and had come home late.

'I'm out in the wilderness somewhere,' replied John. 'But we can meet again another time. I just wanted to hear how things are going with the magic Advent calendar.'

'Fine,' said Joachim. 'It's almost like having a birthday every day, because now Mama and Papa are reading all the pieces of paper too. We do it together.'

'Is that so? It's still possible to read them, then?'

Joachim didn't understand what he meant. 'We read them every day.'

'Fine – yes, that's fine. Where has the pilgrimage got to now?'

'I think it's called Philippi,' replied Joachim. 'We've looked it up on the map.'

'That's good. That was really the point of it too. But Joachim?'

'Yes?'

'What do you think the Greek sheep farmer thought when

he saw the angel-procession going down to the Axios Valley?'

'He must have been very frightened,' said Joachim.

'Yes, you can say that again.'

'But there are a lot of things Mama and Papa want to ask you about,' continued Joachim. 'Can you come to coffee with us?'

John laughed. 'It's not Christmas yet.'

'You can have coffee and cakes just the same. We've baked quite a lot already.'

He was suddenly afraid that John might stop talking, so he hurried to ask, 'Are you sure the lady in the photo is called Elisabet?'

'I'm almost sure,' said John. 'If not, she's called Tebasile.'

Joachim thought of the strange Advent calendar Quirinius had given Elisabet, and of what John had said when they met by the garden gate. 'Perhaps she's called both,' he said. 'Perhaps she's called Elisabet Tebasile.'

There was a long silence.

'Yes, maybe so. Maybe *so*, yes!' said John at last.

'Was she Norwegian?'

'Both yes and no,' said John. 'She was from Palestine, from a little village near Bethlehem. She said she was a Palestinian refugee. But it seems she was born in Norway. The whole thing's so strange.'

'So then she ran to Bethlehem with Ephiriel and the lamb?' asked Joachim. It took his breath away.

'How you ask!' said John. 'But now I must hang up. We must learn to wait, you see, Joachim. Did you know that "Advent" means something that is to come?'

And he put down the receiver.

Joachim couldn't settle to anything at home until Mama

and Papa arrived. He had to tell them about phone call over and over again, for Papa wanted to be quite sure John hadn't said anything important that Joachim had forgotten.

'Elisabet Tebasile!' he muttered. 'There can't be anyone called that.'

But there was something else. Joachim knew that a refugee was someone who had to flee from her own country because of war and danger, but he didn't know that anyone had been forced to flee from Bethlehem.

Papa had to look up the atlas again. He told Joachim that many people in the villages around Bethlehem had had to move out of their own country because of war. Some of them had lost all their possessions and were in such difficulties that they were forced to live in refugee camps.

'A Good Samaritan should have come to help them,' said Joachim. 'Jesus wanted to teach people to help one another when any of them needed it. And then there would have been peace. For peace is the message of Christmas.'

the
EIGHTEENTH
OF DECEMBER

. . . God's kingdom is open to everyone, even people

who travel without a ticket . . .

PAPA HADN'T LIKED Joachim opening the magic Advent calendar before he and Mama got up. On the eighteenth of December it was he who woke Joachim.

That day there was a picture of a rod with a shining gold ball on one end.

'That's a sceptre,' explained Mama. 'Kings and emperors have used rods like that as a symbol of dignity. The round ball is probably meant to be the sun.'

Joachim unfolded the little piece of paper that had fallen out of the calendar and read aloud to Mama and Papa. They sat on each side of him on his bed.

THE EMPEROR AUGUSTUS

A STRANGE PROCESSION SWEPT through Thrace towards Constantinople on their way to Bethlehem. Five hundred years had passed since Jesus was born in a stable, swaddled in a piece of cloth, and placed in a manger because there was no room for Mary and Joseph in the inn. But that old story was already familiar in large areas of the world.

They stopped in front of one of the city gates that was guarded by soldiers. The soldiers drew their swords and raised their spears as soon as the first sheep reached the gate. Then the angel Seraphiel flew up beside the sheep and placed himself between them and the soldiers.

'Be not afraid,' he said. 'We are on our way to Bethlehem to pay homage to the Christ-child. You must allow us to pass.'

The soldiers dropped their weapons and threw themselves on the ground. One of them signalled that they could pass through the city gate. Soon all the pilgrims were inside the solid city walls.

It was early in the morning, and the city was not yet awake. The procession of pilgrims stopped on a hill with a good view of the harbour and the Bosporus which divides Europe from Asia. The sound was so narrow that they could see across to the other side.

'The time is 495,' said Ephiriel. 'Originally the city was called Byzantium, but in the year of Our Lord 330 it was made the capital of the Roman Empire by the Emperor Constantine. First he called the city New Rome, but it was soon given the name Constantinople. After that the city took back the old Greek name, Byzantium. In just under a thousand years, in 1453, the city will be conquered by the Turks, and they will give it the name Istanbul.'

'Had the soldiers heard about Jesus?' Elisabet wanted to know.

'We can take that for granted. The Emperor Constantine made Christianity a lawful religion in the Roman Empire as early as 313. He was baptised himself just before he died. Some years later, in 380, Christianity became the state religion throughout the Roman Empire.'

'However do you manage to remember all the dates?' asked Elisabet.

'I only have to follow the angel watch,' replied Ephiriel. 'Since we don't have to bother about all those seconds, minutes, hours and days, it's not so difficult to remember the years. Another date we must notice is the year 395, exactly a hundred years ago. That was when the Roman Empire was divided, and Constantinople became the capital of the Eastern Roman Empire.'

The angel Seraphiel came up. He pointed at a beautiful church.

'That church is called a basilica,' he said, 'and was built in honour of God's wisdom by the Emperor Constantine. In a few years it will be destroyed by fire, but on the same spot the lovely Santa Sophia church will be built. It will stand as a landmark for centuries.'

'We must get across the Bosporus,' said Quirinius. 'Then it's not very far to Syria. Dixi!'

Joshua thumped his shepherd's crook on the ground.

'To Bethlehem! To Bethlehem!'

They ran down through the city and before long were standing on the furthest point of the Golden Horn. At the edge of the quay they were met by a magnificent man in colourful clothes and with a glittering sceptre in his hand. In the other hand he was holding a thick book.

Impuriel was already airborne in order to say 'Fear not', but the handsome man took no notice of the cherub. He came straight towards them.

'I am the Emperor Augustus and I shall accompany you across the Bosporus. I order you to accept this gesture without any unpleasant protests.'

He showed them a boat with several large sails. The sheep had already begun to jump on board.

'Then you are one of us,' said Ephiriel.

Elisabet turned to the angel and said, 'I didn't know the Emperor Augustus was a Christian.'

A mysterious smile passed over the angel's face.

'But the old Roman Emperor has been taking part in the Christmas gospel as a kind of stowaway for many centuries. And God's kingdom is open to everyone, even people who travel without a ticket.'

Elisabet thought the angel's words made heaven even bigger than she had imagined. She hid what he had said in her heart.

Soon the large company were over on the other side of the Bosporus. As they landed, Elisabet greeted the Roman Emperor and asked what kind of book he had under his arm. She thought he was going to say it was the Bible, or at any rate a hymn book, for heaven could surely demand this much of an old emperor who had suddenly decided to go along with them to Bethlehem. But the Emperor Augustus said, 'It is the sacred census.'

He said no more. He was so handsome and so proud that he clearly did not like talking for too long at a time, at any rate not to little girls. Elisabet thought that was a bit odd, for it surely didn't happen every day that a Roman emperor was able to greet a girl who had run off after a lamb who had escaped from a store in Norway and headed for Bethlehem.

Joshua struck the ground with his crook and reminded them where they were going. But they hadn't run very far before they stopped on a hill above the town of Chalcedon.

The town was teeming with priests: they were like a swarm of bees. Elisabet was astonished, in fact almost scared, to see so many priests at once.

'Fear not,' said the angel Seraphiel. 'The time is 451 years after the birth of Jesus, and the biggest conference in the history of the Christian Church is being held down there. The town is called Chalcedon, and priests and bishops from the whole of the Christian world have poured in.'

'What are they talking about?' Elisabet wanted to know.

The angel laughed. 'They're trying to reach agreement about correct Christian doctrine.'

'Are they going to agree?'

'After long discussions they'll finally make a declaration that says that Jesus was both God and man. But they're discussing a great deal else as well. Some of them are so eager to find out what is the correct belief that in their haste they forget what is most important.'

'And what's that?' asked Elisabet.

'That Jesus came into the world to teach people to be kind to one another. No other lesson is more difficult for a human being to learn, or more important. It's not as important to know how many angels there are in heaven or whether God has a splinter in His little finger.'

'Has he *really* got one?'

'It doesn't matter, I told you. It's more important to see the beam in your own eye.'

Elisabet found that very difficult to understand, but she hid the angel's words in her heart. Perhaps she would understand them better another time.

The two Wise Men were clearly not entirely satisfied with what the angel had said.

'It is, strictly speaking, not necessary to believe in angels at all,' said Caspar. 'Many people believe that such concepts have very little to do with what Jesus wished to teach us.'

'The angel stories may only be fairy stories,' added Balthazar. 'But that Jesus wished to teach humans to be kind to one another was no fairy story.'

Only now did Ephiriel begin to argue.

'We angels are not used to using such strong words,' he said in a gentle voice. 'All the same, I must say that this is one of the silliest things I've ever heard, at least on this pilgrimage. You should be ashamed of yourselves, both of you. Or you should stay in the Orient and not start wandering westwards with such irresponsible talk.'

'Yes, indeed,' added Impuriel. 'You should be ashamed of yourselves, both of you. I'm offended.'

The next moment Impuriel did something Elisabet thought angels in heaven would never do. He put his hand in front of his offended face and thumbed his nose at the two Wise Men from the Orient!

'Bah to you!' said the cherub. 'Yes, indeed!'

A certain nervousness began to spread among the godly company. The angel Seraphiel unfolded his arms to show he was not carrying any weapons.

'It's easy to lose courage when even your nearest and dearest lose faith in you. But although we can disagree about such important matters of belief, we mustn't under any circumstances begin to quarrel. Now let's try to forget the unkind things that have been said and the unkindness that was thumbed.'

Joshua the shepherd was clearly in agreement with the last speaker, for now he thumped his crook on the ground and said, 'To Bethlehem! To Bethlehem!'

And with that they started moving down through Phrygia.

JOACHIM SIGHED HEAVILY and let the piece of paper fall into his lap.

'It's silly when grown-ups quarrel,' he said, 'but it's even sillier when the angels in heaven start quarrelling.'

Papa nodded. 'These have always been sensitive matters. It's not the first time people have got cross because of a discussion about angels.'

'But they didn't disagree so very much,' protested Mama. 'The angels and the Wise Men agreed that the most important lesson Jesus wanted to teach people was that we ought to be kind to one another. And that can, in fact, be much more difficult than believing in angels.'

Papa opened the atlas and pointed out Constantinople, which is called Istanbul today; also the narrow Bosporus Strait where the Emperor Augustus had taken them across by boat.

In the pancake book he found the old city of Chalcedon where all the priests had met in order to discuss what Christian doctrine was. Now the pilgrims had arrived in Asia.

When Mama came home from work that afternoon she had a large envelope full of newspaper articles. She had been to the library to get copies of everything that had been written in the newspapers when Elisabet Hansen disappeared in 1948.

The family sat round the coffee table, reading the old newspaper cuttings. They examined the picture of Elisabet Hansen carefully. Mama took down the photo of

the grown-up Elisabet from the mantelpiece and began to
compare the pictures. Could the two pictures be of one and
the same Elisabet?

'Both of them have fair hair,' said Mama. 'And I think
they've both got a slightly pointed nose too.'

'Impossible to tell!' snorted Papa.

He was more interested in the disappearance. As he read
the old newspapers he said, 'Her mother was a teacher …
her father was a well-known journalist … only her little
knitted hat was found when the snow melted a few months
later, in some woodland. Otherwise the police had no clues
at all.'

'*They* hadn't read the magic Advent calendar,' said
Joachim.

'Even if they had, they couldn't have arrested an angel,'
laughed Papa.

After Joachim went to bed later that evening and Mama
and Papa had said goodnight, he put the light on again. It
occurred to him that he hadn't looked at the large picture
on the outside of the Advent calendar for several days. That
was because most of the doors in the calendar had been
opened. So he closed them.

THEN IT HAPPENED AGAIN!

The picture showed Mary and Joseph leaning over the
baby Jesus in the manger. In the background were the Wise
Men, and the angels descending through the clouds to tell
the shepherds in the fields that Jesus was born.

High up on the left side there was a picture of two men in
fine clothes. Unlike all the others they were standing with
their backs to the scene. Joachim had seen them before, and
now he was quite certain that they were supposed to be
Quirinius and the Emperor Augustus. But only at this

moment did he notice that the Emperor was carrying a shining sceptre. Had he been holding a sceptre in his hand ever since Joachim was given the magic Advent calendar in the little bookshop?

Or had the sceptre drawn itself in?

the
NINETEENTH
OF DECEMBER

. . . he thought it was such fun to throw gifts

through people's windows . . .

O N THE NINETEENTH of December there was a picture of a Christmas *nisse* in the magic Advent calendar. He had long white hair and a white beard and was wearing a red cloak and a pointed red hat. On his chest hung a large silver cross set with a red stone.

Mama read what was on the little piece of paper in the Advent calendar.

MELCHIOR

A PROCESSION WAS SPEEDING through Asia Minor one day towards the end of the fourth century. They travelled across the high plains of Phrygia and passed some salt lakes where the birds can stand on the water. On their long journey they encountered bears, wolves and jackals, but when a wolf or a bear came running towards them, they always managed to step aside by one or two weeks and avoid it.

They climbed up through a pass in the high mountain range of Pamphylia, which stretches from east to west along the Mediterranean coast. A couple of thousand metres above sea level they caught sight of a figure dressed in green. It was a tall man, sitting like a living landmark at the watershed where the road began tilting downwards towards the Mediterranean Sea.

As soon as they noticed the figure in green Caspar and Balthazar began waving their arms and tried to run past the sheep.

'Who's that?' asked Elisabet.

'He must certainly be one of us,' said the angel Ephiriel.

The stranger rose and threw his arms round Caspar and Balthazar.

'The circle is complete,' he announced solemnly.

Elisabet didn't understand this, but then the stranger came over and greeted her politely as well.

'Welcome to Pamphylia,' he said. 'My name is Melchior, Third Wise Man and King of Egriskulla.'

Then Elisabet understood what he had meant by the circle being complete, for now all three Kings of Orient were gathered together.

'You have so many strange names,' she said. 'You're Wise Men, Kings of Orient, and Caspar, Balthazar and Melchior.'

Melchior smiled from ear to ear.

'We have still more names. In Greek we are called Galagat, Magalat and Sakarin. Other people call us Magi. But it doesn't matter what they call us. We are part of this story on behalf of all people on earth who do not come from the Holy Land.'

Elisabet looked up at the angel Ephiriel, and the angel nodded.

'That's quite true.'

'Of course. One would not tell lies, surely?' continued Melchior. 'One would not have been a King of Orient unless one spoke the truth, surely? One would not have been particularly wise, either, only seeming-wise.'

He was so funny when he talked that Elisabet couldn't help laughing. He had more to say.

'Besides, I wouldn't have been called Melchior if I hadn't been fond of milk. Nor would I have been called Sakarin unless I was fond of sugar. In short, I am so happy that I often want to sing and dance. And I am always very happy every Christmas Eve, for that's when Jesus was born.'

'That'll do,' said Joshua, striking a stone with his shepherd's crook. 'To Bethlehem! To Bethlehem!'

But Melchior spoke again. 'We must greet the Christmas *nisse* first. He lives just below here.'

With which they set off down the steep mountainsides towards the Mediterranean Sea. While they ran, Elisabet said, 'Is it really true that we're going to greet the Christmas *nisse*?'

Ephiriel pointed down at a town clinging to the side of the mountain. They could glimpse the Mediterranean in the background.

'The time is 322. The town is called Myra, and this is where Paul came when he was travelling to Rome to tell the capital of the Roman Empire about Jesus. He founded a Christian community in Myra too.'

'I don't understand what that has to do with the Christmas *nisse*.'

But the angel went on, 'Two hundred years after Paul came to Myra a boy was born here who was called Nicholas. His parents were Christians, and later on Nicholas was elected Bishop of Myra. In Myra there lived a girl who was very poor because her father had lost everything he owned. She wanted to get married, but it was quite impossible because she had no money for her dowry. Bishop Nicholas wanted to help the poor girl, but he knew her family were too proud to accept a gift of money.'

'Perhaps he could have put some money into her father's bank account,' suggested Elisabet.

'Yes, although this was a long time before such things as banks existed. But Nicholas did something similar. He crept out during the night and threw a bag of gold coins through their open window. In that way the girl got the money to marry after all.'

'That was kind of him.'

'But it didn't stop there. He thought it was such fun to throw gifts through people's windows that he went on doing it. When he died, many legends were told about him. Later he became St Nicholas. That turned into Santa Claus, and in Norwegian into the Christmas *nisse*. The word *nisse* comes from Nicholas, and so do the names Nils and Klaus.'

'Did he have red clothes, a long white beard and a red hat?'

'Wait and see,' said the angel Ephiriel.

The sun had not yet risen. They stopped in front of a low church building in Myra.

As soon as they stopped the church door opened. Out strode a magnificent man with a long red cloak, a long white beard, and a red hat. Round his neck he wore a large silver cross with a red stone in it. He almost looked like a Christmas *nisse*, but Ephiriel whispered in Elisabet's ear that the time was 325 years after the birth of Jesus and that the man was dressed in quite normal bishop's clothes. Only later was the red robe of the bishop exchanged for black clothes in some places.

'It is Bishop Nicholas of Myra,' whispered the angel.

Elisabet had an idea. 'Has it anything to do with myrrh?'

'You do well to say so, for myrrh was one of the three Christmas gifts to the Christ-child,' said the angel with a smile. 'It's become the custom to give gifts at Christmas because of the gifts the Three Wise Men brought to the Christ-child, and because of Bishop Nicholas's generosity.'

In his arms the man held three different caskets. He walked firmly towards the Three Kings of Orient, bowed low, and offered each of them a casket. Caspar's casket was full of shining gold coins. In Balthazar's casket was incense, and in Melchior's casket myrrh.

'We are on our way to Bethlehem,' said Caspar.

Bishop Nicholas laughed so that his beard shook.

'Ho, ho! So you must take a few little gifts for the Child in the manger. You simply must do that, mustn't you? Ho, ho!'

Since Elisabet was standing in front of a real Christmas *nisse*, she ran right up to him and felt his red cloak. Then he bent down and lifted her up on his arm. She tried to pull his beard to find out whether it was real, and it was.

'Why are you so kind?' she asked.

'Ho, ho!' laughed the man in red again. 'The more we give away, the richer we become, and the more we keep for ourselves, the poorer we become. That's the mystery of generosity, neither more nor less. But it's the mystery of poverty too.'

The angel Impuriel clapped his hands. 'Well spoken, Bishop!'

Bishop Nicholas continued, 'All those who lay up for themselves treasures upon earth will be poor one day, but those who have given away all they possess will never be poor. Besides, they have had great fun. Ho, ho! For the greatest joy on earth is generosity.'

'That may be so,' said Elisabet, 'but first you must own something to give away.'

At that the good-natured Bishop laughed so violently that

his whole body shook. Elisabet almost felt seasick as she sat on his arm.

'Not at all,' he said, when he had swallowed enough of his laughter that there was room in his mouth for speaking as well. 'You needn't own anything at all to feel generosity fizzing in your veins. A little smile is enough, or something you've made yourself.'

And with those words he put Elisabet down again on the mosaic floor in front of the church.

Joshua thumped his shepherd's crook on the ground.

'To Bethlehem! To Bethlehem!'

As they moved off they could hear the Bishop's laughter behind them in the church square.

'Ho-ho! Ho-ho! Ho-ho!'

MAMA LOOKED UP from the paper and began laughing as well. It was infectious, and when Joachim burst out laughing, Papa couldn't resist it either. So they sat there chuckling, all three of them.

At last Mama said, 'I think laughter is like the wild flowers. Both are a part of the glory of heaven that has strayed down to earth. But that kind of thing is easily scattered.'

Before Mama had finished reading what was written on the scrap of paper, Papa had brought out the historical atlas.

'The names are on the map,' he said. 'And Paul really did visit a little town called Myra when he was on his way from Jerusalem to Rome.'

'Perhaps Elisabet in the photo travelled the same way as Paul,' suggested Joachim, 'because she went to Rome too.'

'And she had a silver cross with a red stone in it,' said Mama. 'The Christmas *nisse* did as well.'

Papa laughed. Then he went into the sitting room to fetch an encyclopedia. He came back, reading as he came down the passage.

'Quite correct about the Bishop of Myra. He was the very first Santa Claus.'

'I must say, history is full of strange connections,' said Mama. 'It's as if small *nisser* have been jumping up and down all through the centuries.'

the
TWENTIETH
OF DECEMBER

. . . something suddenly fell out of the sky . . .

ON SUNDAY THE twentieth of December Joachim was woken by the alarm clock in Mama and Papa's bedroom. They hardly ever set the alarm for Sundays, and Joachim thought they were afraid he would wake up and open the magic Advent calendar without them. At any rate, the next moment they were both in their usual places.

'So let's get going,' said Papa.

Joachim opened the door with the number 20 on it. There was a picture of a man lying on the ground, looking up at a bright light that was shining down from heaven.

'What a curious picture,' said Mama.

But Papa was impatient. 'Let's start reading,' he said. Today it was his turn to unfold the little piece of paper and read aloud from the very tiny writing.

CHERUBIEL

A PROCESSION WAS on its way through Asia Minor. During the third century it sped through Pamphylia and Cilicia south of the high Taurus mountains, crossing rivers, orchards and plateaux. Sometimes the pilgrims made their way along steep slopes with old rock graves; sometimes they floundered along the edge of the beach so that the sand spurted up around them; sometimes they sped through Roman cities such as Attalia, Seleucia and Tarsus. At Tarsus they paused and looked around for a few seconds. The angel Ephiriel told them that it was Paul's birthplace.

On their journey the pilgrims passed Roman theatres, sports stadia, harbours, triumphal arches and temples. Now and again they saw something that might have been a Christian church.

The route was planned so that they should not attract too much attention. It took them a century to cross the country but they showed themselves only in the grey light of dawn before people had woken up. Here and there they frightened the wits out of a night watchman, or a fisherman who was setting out his nets early. As a rule they sped on, and the poor man would be left standing rubbing his eyes, but sometimes the angel Impuriel called out that he should not be afraid.

For a human being doesn't often see one of the angels of the Lord, and even then the sight doesn't last longer than a second or two. Then it's easy to believe you've seen visions, especially if you're a poor night watchman who hasn't closed his eyes during the long hours of his spell of duty.

The mysterious procession sped round the Gulf of Alexandretta at the very end of the Mediterranean Sea. From now on the way to Bethlehem went south along the eastern coast of the Mediterranean. They arrived at the Syrian city of Antioch and stopped in front of the town gate.

'We are in the year of Our Lord 238,' said Ephiriel. 'This is where Paul's first missionary journeys began. We ought to remember, too, that the word "Christian" was used for the first time in Antioch.'

'But weren't Jesus's disciples Christian?' Elisabet wanted to know.

'Yes and no,' replied Ephiriel. 'It took a long time for the first Christians to begin calling themselves Christians, and the first occasion when that happened was in this very city. Before then the Christians thought of themselves as Jews. Paul was a Jew too, but on his missionary journeys he found out that Romans and Greeks could also believe in Jesus. Paul thought they didn't need to become Jews before they began to believe in Jesus. They didn't need to follow all the old rules in the laws of Moses either. Because Jesus didn't talk to the Jews alone. He had something to say to all people.'

The Wise Men came up beside Ephiriel.

'We are Wise Men from the Orient,' said Caspar, 'and Kings of Nubia, Sheba and Egriskulla. None of us has a drop of Jewish blood in our veins, but all the same, we are among the very first to welcome the Christ-child into the world.'

Joshua struck his shepherd's crook against the city wall.

'To Bethlehem!' he said. 'To Bethlehem!'

The procession of pilgrims moved off on their way to Damascus, the capital of Syria.

After a while Ephiriel called to them to stop. They were on a deserted stretch of the old Roman road through Syria.

'Here it is,' said Ephiriel, pointing at a bright red poppy at the side of the road. He continued, 'The time is 235 years after the birth of Jesus. Two hundred years ago a miracle took place here, and it was of great importance for the history of the whole world.'

The Three Wise Men lined up and bowed solemnly, and to show that he agreed, the Emperor Augustus planted his sceptre on the spot the angel had indicated.

The four shepherds tried to collect the little flock of sheep round the Emperor's sceptre. It shone like a small sun. Quirinius called their attention to the landscape and said, 'It's good to be home again. Now it's only a couple of hundred years since I was the Governor of Syria. Dixi.'

'Excuse me for asking you so directly,' said Elisabet, 'but I may be the only person who doesn't understand what you're all talking about. Jesus wasn't born here, was he?'

Ephiriel laughed.

'In the year of Our Lord 35 after Christ a Jew from Tarsus in Asia Minor was on his way to Damascus. His Roman name was Paul, but his Jewish name was Saul. As a young man he had lived in Jerusalem where he studied the ancient Jewish scriptures. He may have met Jesus there and listened to what He had to say. But Paul was a Pharisee, and the Pharisees believed that people could keep in with God by following all the laws and precepts in the Books of Moses. He became one of the enthusiastic persecutors of the Christians. He helped to throw them in prison, and even helped to kill St Stephen.'

'Then he was stupid,' said Elisabet.

Ephiriel and all the others nodded. The angel continued, 'But when he was on his way to Damascus to persecute the Christians there, he had a strange experience. Suddenly a light shone down from heaven, and Paul heard a voice saying, "Saul, Saul, why do you persecute me?" Paul asked who was calling him, and the answer was, "I am Jesus, whom you are persecuting. Get up and go into the city, and you will be told what you have to do." Paul and the men who were with him were struck speechless. All of them had heard the voice speaking, but none of them had seen anything but the light from heaven.'

'That's exactly how it was,' said Impuriel. 'The voice they heard didn't even say, "Fear not".'

'Paul went into Damascus and joined the congregation

there. Before long he became the first great Christian missionary. Paul was a Roman citizen, he spoke Greek, and Aramaic which was the language Jesus spoke. And he could read the scrolls of scripture in Hebrew. On his four missionary journeys he preached about Jesus in Greece and Rome, Syria and Asia Minor.'

While Ephiriel was speaking something suddenly fell out of the sky. It happened so quickly that Elisabet didn't even have time to jump. At first she thought it was a bird that had fallen to earth because it had forgotten to beat its wings. Then she saw that a new angel was standing in front of her.

'Fear not,' said the angel. 'I am Cherubiel and I shall accompany you on the last stage of your journey to Bethlehem.'

The Emperor Augustus picked up the sceptre that had stood where Paul had heard the voice from heaven, the shepherds gave the sheep a little push, and Joshua exclaimed, 'To Bethlehem! To Bethlehem!'

PAPA LET THE piece of paper fall on to the bed. 'Incredible!' he said.

He opened the atlas which showed how the country they travelled through had looked in the third century after Christ. Then he repeated all the names and pointed at the map. It was almost as if he was singing them: 'Pamphylia, Cilicia, Attalia, Seleucia, Tarsus and Antioch.'

Since it was Sunday they had plenty of time. They had already begun getting ready for Christmas: washing clothes and floors, baking cakes and colouring marzipan sweets.

That day Mama and Papa did nothing but read old atlases and encyclopedias. They wanted to know about the places the pilgrims had passed through.

'I feel as if I'm back at school,' laughed Mama.

Papa read aloud from a book in the Bible called the Acts of the Apostles, where there was a lot about Paul.

'I've found it here,' he said. ' "While he was still on the road and nearing Damascus, suddenly a light flashed from the sky all around him. He fell to the ground and heard a voice saying, 'Saul, Saul, why do you persecute me?' 'Tell me, Lord,' he said, 'who you are.' The voice answered, 'I am Jesus, whom you are persecuting. But get up and go into the city, and you will be told what you have to do.' Meanwhile the men who were travelling with him stood speechless; they heard the voice but could see no one. Saul got up from the ground, but when he opened his eyes he could not see; so they led him by the hand and brought him into Damascus. He was blind for three days, and took no food or drink." '

It was strange for Joachim to see Papa sitting in the green rocking chair, reading the Bible. Once he put the heavy book down in his lap and said, 'This book is really quite as remarkable as the magic Advent calendar.'

As Joachim was eating his supper the phone rang. Mama took it and gave the receiver to Papa.

'Yes,' he said. 'Speaking ... of course it happened years ago. No, I understand that ... Yes, it's a clear picture ... Quite certain. It's St Peter's in the background ... I would never have given up hope either ... no, I wouldn't ... All we have is this strange calendar that came to us by accident ... He's disappeared ... No, I've never met him ... My family say that too ... pointed nose, yes ... No, I don't believe in angels, not at all ... Of course it's possible that she was kidnapped ... no, but somebody or other ... I don't know, but it's clearly possible that she's still alive. She'd be unlikely to remember anything ... she was only seven. Not even that, you say? ... We have just the one boy ... no, I would never have given up hope ... At once, yes, I promise, and thank you for ringing.'

He put down the receiver.

'Was that John?' asked Joachim.

'It was Mrs Hansen, Elisabet's mother,' said Papa. 'I sent her a copy of that old photo. She said the young woman could well be her daughter who disappeared, but then she was only six or seven years old. She had another daughter immediately afterwards. Her name's Anna, and she looks a little like the young woman in front of St Peter's ...'

When Papa came in to say goodnight that evening, he stood for a while with his back to Joachim, staring into the darkness outside the window.

'What on earth do you think has happened to John?'

'He's out in the wilderness,' said Joachim. 'But it's not Christmas yet.'

the
TWENTY-
FIRST
OF DECEMBER

. . . the lake looked like a blue china bowl,

edged with gold . . .

PAPA WOKE JOACHIM early on the morning of Monday, the twenty-first of December.

'We must hurry up and get going,' he said. 'I have to go to work a bit early today, you see. But this is important too, maybe even more important than my job.'

Joachim sat up in bed and opened the Advent calendar. He had almost begun to dread Christmas because then there wouldn't be anything left of the calendar.

That day there was a picture of a village beside a shining lake. The village and the low hills round the lake were bathed in gold.

Joachim unfolded the little piece of paper that had fallen out of the calendar when he opened it, and read aloud.

EVANGELIEL

EARLY ONE MORNING at the end of the second century after Christ the companions tumbled at top speed into Damascus on the bank of the River Barada. They sped past two soldiers who were guarding the western gate and sprang in along the straight street that cuts right through the city.

The soldiers turned to one another in confusion.

'What was that?'

'Only a gust of wind from the north-west.'

'But it wasn't just wind and sand. I thought I saw people as well.'

The two soldiers were reminded of an old story from a few years ago, about something that had happened at the eastern gate. A group of soldiers had been knocked over by a procession that had approached along the main street and thundered out through the city gate. It had consisted of people and animals, and one of the soldiers thought he had seen angels as well.

For as Elisabet, Ephiriel and all the others rushed out through the eastern city gate, they happened to bump into some Roman soldiers. The soldiers fell down, picked themselves up in confusion and tried to see where they had gone. But the procession was soon many years and miles away.

Late in the afternoon one day in the middle of the second century they came down to the Lake of Gennesareth in Galilee. They stopped in front of a village and looked out across the shining water.

The hills lay like a wreath round the lake, and now that the golden evening sun was shining on them, Elisabet thought the lake looked like a blue china bowl, edged with gold.

The village consisted of simple houses with a small shed for livestock at one end. Between the houses walked loaded donkeys led by men wearing tunics and cloaks. The women, in loose clothing, were carrying jars on their heads.

'We are in Capernaum, which is on the old caravan trail between Damascus and Egypt,' explained Ephiriel. 'Here Jesus called His first disciples. One of them was the customs official, Matthew, for Capernaum was an important customs station. Others were the brothers Simon Peter and Andrew, who were both fishermen. "Follow me," said Jesus, "and I will make you fishers of men."'

'He helped them to catch ordinary fish too,' Impuriel hastened to add.

Ephiriel nodded.

'Once when Jesus was standing beside the lake to speak to a large crowd of people, He caught sight of two boats lying further down the beach. One of them belonged to Simon Peter. Jesus went on board Peter's boat and asked him to put out from the land. Then He sat in the boat and talked to the crowd from the lake. That was a good idea, because then all the people could see Him while he spoke. When He had finished speaking He asked Simon Peter to row further out and cast his nets there. Peter said he had tried to catch fish all night without getting a single one. All the same, he did as Jesus said, and then he caught so many fish that the net broke with the weight of them.'

'Another time they were out on the lake,' said Impuriel. 'Suddenly a storm blew up, and the disciples were terrified of drowning, but Jesus simply lay down and slept. In the end He was forced to quieten the storm in order to calm the disciples.'

'He wanted to show them that they had very little faith,' explained Ephiriel.

'Yes, indeed!' said Impuriel vigorously. 'Yet another time the disciples were out on the lake alone when Jesus came towards them, walking on the water. When the disciples saw Him they were scared, because they thought He was a ghost. But when Simon Peter saw it was Jesus, he thought he'd show off a bit to prove how much faith he had. So he stepped out of the boat and walked on the water too. It went well at first, but soon he grew afraid of the waves and began to sink. He called to Jesus and asked Him to come and save him.'

Joshua struck his shepherd's crook against a heap of broken stones.

'To Bethlehem! To Bethlehem!'

They sped off along the shore of the Lake of Gennesareth. Before long Ephiriel called to them to stop. He pointed up at a shelf in the rock.

'That's where Jesus gave the famous Sermon on the Mount. He talked about the most important things He wanted to teach us.'

'So what were they?' Elisabet wanted to know.

The cherub Impuriel spread his wings, jumped up in the air and said, 'Our Father, Who art in heaven! Hallowed be Thy name. Thy Kingdom come. Thy will be done on earth as it is in heaven . . .'

Here he was interrupted by Ephiriel.

'Yes, He taught them to pray. Above all, He wanted to teach human beings to be kind to one another. He also wanted to show that nobody is perfect in the sight of God.'

' "Blessed are the merciful," ' said Impuriel. ' "Whosoever shall smite thee on thy right cheek, turn to him the other also . . . Love your enemies and pray for those who persecute you . . . whatsoever ye would that men should do to you, do ye even so unto them . . ." '

'That's enough, thank you!' interrupted Ephiriel. 'We know you remember it all. And I should think so too, as one of the angels of the Lord.'

All three Wise Men clearly wanted to say something. Caspar and Balthazar nodded at Melchior and let him speak.

'But it's not enough to learn such rules of life by heart. It's more important to try to follow them. The most important thing is to do something for people in need, for people who are ill and poor, and for people fleeing from their homes. That is the message of Christmas.'

'To Bethlehem!' attempted Joshua again. 'To Bethlehem!'

They had scarcely got up speed when Ephiriel turned to Elisabet and told her that they were running through the area where Jesus had fed five thousand people with only a few loaves and fishes.

'Yes, indeed!' said Impuriel. 'Jesus wanted people to share the little they had. If only they could learn to share with each other, nobody would be hungry or poor, or very rich either. But it's better that nobody is poor and hungry than that a few people are rich.'

When they came to the village of Tiberias they turned away from the Lake of Gennesareth, up through a hilly landscape. At the head of a fertile valley with palms and fruit trees stood another village. Ephiriel called to the procession to stop.

'Angel time says 107 years have passed since Jesus was born. This town is called Nazareth. Jesus grew up here as the son of Joseph the carpenter. It was here that one of the angels of the Lord appeared to Mary and told her she was going to have a child.'

He had scarcely finished speaking when something seemed to fall down through a hole in the sky. The next moment yet another angel was standing in front of the procession. In his hand he held a trumpet. The angel blew once on the trumpet and said, 'I am the angel Evangeliel, and I proclaim to you a great joy. There is only a short time left until Jesus is born.'

Impuriel began fluttering around Elisabet.

'He is one of us and will be with us on the last part of our
journey to Bethlehem.'

What had happened reminded Elisabet of the words from
the old Christmas carol.

> ' "The angel of the Lord came down
> And glory shone around," '

she sang in as pretty a voice as she could.

The Three Wise Men clapped their hands because she sang
so beautifully.

That embarrassed her. So that they shouldn't all look at
her, she said, 'I can see we must be getting close to Bethlehem
if there are so many angels here.'

Joshua gave one of the sheep a little slap on its rump.

'To Bethlehem! To Bethlehem!'

Now there were only a hundred years to go before they
reached the city of David.

PAPA HAD SAT staring in front of him while Joachim
read the last lines from the piece of paper.

'Now things are starting to fall into place,' he said.

'You mean, they've arrived in the Holy Land?' said Mama.

Papa shook his head. 'Quirinius said something yesterday
when they were approaching Damascus. "It's good to be
home again," he said. Naturally that was because the Governor of Syria may have lived in Damascus at one time. But
I seem to hear John's voice: "It's good to be home again".'

'You mean John made the magic Advent calendar, and he
really does come from Damascus?' asked Mama.

Papa nodded. 'For who is Quirinius in this extraordinary story? It was Quirinius who gave Elisabet an Advent calendar, the one with the picture of the fair-haired girl. That's how he's imagined himself into the story he's telling, himself and the young woman he met in Rome. He's put it into the middle of this long story, because although Quirinius and the Advent calendar only come into the twelfth and thirteenth chapters, Quirinius has said "Dixi" all the time when he has had something to say. That means, "I have spoken" – and I can hear John's voice again. He has spoken, and what he has said is in this remarkable Advent calendar. But an interesting bit of information came out today.'

'What's that?' asked Mama and Joachim together.

'The old flower-seller has described many towns and places on the long journey to Bethlehem, but today the description was more exact. He writes about the straight street that cuts right through Damascus from the western to the eastern gate. Only someone who's familiar with the place would write like that.'

'Perhaps you're right,' said Mama. 'But don't you think he may really have heard the old story about the soldiers who were knocked over by a procession of angels?'

'Nonsense!' snorted Papa. Then he stopped himself. 'But nothing can be discounted. If only we could find him again!'

Joachim was thinking about something quite different. He looked down at the piece of paper that he'd been reading from, put his finger on one of the sentences and said, 'The Wise Man said it's important to do something for people who are fleeing from their homes. What do you think he meant by that?'

'I suppose he was thinking of refugees and people like that,' said Papa.

'Exactly!' said Joachim. 'That's just what I thought.'

'What do you mean?' asked Mama.

'I thought it had something to do with the lady in the photo. *She* was a refugee too. Besides, she was his girlfriend.'

Papa got to his feet. 'We'd better hurry,' he said. 'I have to be off in ten minutes.'

Before Joachim fell asleep that evening he sat for a while playing with the letters of the alphabet. He thought about John who had met Elisabet in Rome, and about Rome that turned into a word for love when he read it backwards.

Finally he wrote some magic letters in his notebook:

```
E L I S A B E T
L             E
I   R O M A   B
S   O     M   A
A   M     O   S
B   A M O R   I
E             L
T E B A S I L E
```

The diagram looked like a door – or perhaps a door that was inside another door. But what was inside *that* door?

the
TWENTY-
SECOND
OF DECEMBER

... his food was locusts and wild honey ...

JOACHIM WOKE UP early on the morning of the twenty-second of December. There were only three days left to Christmas – and only three doors left to open in the magic Advent calendar. He was excited about what he would learn, but he didn't dare begin before his mother and father got up.

There they were, both of them. Papa seemed almost nervous.

'We'd better get going.'

Joachim opened the door and saw a picture of a man standing in a river that reached up to his waist. The upper part of his body was clothed in rags.

Mama unfolded the piece of paper and read.

THE INNKEEPER

A GODLY BAND were journeying through Samaria. It was at the very end of the first century after Jesus's birth. They were going to Bethlehem, to Bethlehem!

In the grey dawn one day in the year 91 they stopped at the bank of the River Jordan, which runs from the Lake of Gennesareth to the Dead Sea.

'Here it is!' called Ephiriel.

The angel Seraphiel took up the story.

'Out here in the wilderness Jesus was baptised by John the Baptist. The Baptist was clad in a cloak of camel hair with a leather belt round his waist. His food was locusts and wild honey.'

'I know that,' said Impuriel, 'for John had said, "There is one to come who is mightier than I. I am not fit to unfasten his sandals. I have baptised you with water, but He will baptise you with the Holy Spirit." Then Jesus came and allowed himself to be baptised in the River Jordan. I was sitting high up above in the clouds, clapping my hands. It was a great moment.'

'Wasn't that when the dove came down from heaven?' Elisabet wanted to know. She thought she had once heard something like that.

Impuriel beat his wings and nodded. 'Yes, indeed!'

'To Bethlehem!' said Joshua. 'To Bethlehem!'

'How far is it to Bethlehem?' asked Elisabet.

'Not very far at all!' said Impuriel.

They began running again and were soon passing a large city. As they ran, Ephiriel said that the city was called Jericho and was possibly the oldest city in the whole world.

They hurried on along the ancient road between Jericho and Jerusalem. It was the road where the Good Samaritan had helped the poor man who fell among thieves.

They stormed up to Jerusalem. First they climbed up to the Mount of Olives. They looked down at Gethsemane where Jesus had been taken prisoner by the Jews, and his disciples had slept when they ought to have been praying for Him. When they looked out over Jerusalem, Elisabet could see only ruined and destroyed buildings. Could this be the Jewish capital?

'The angel watch says it's the year 71 after Christ,'

explained Ephiriel. 'Barely a year ago the Romans sacked Jerusalem and destroyed the city because its people had rebelled against the Roman colonial power. Today the Eternal City is like a shattered piece of pottery.'

'It was the Emperor Titus who did it,' said Impuriel. 'Not just him alone, of course. It was Titus and tens of thousands of soldiers.'

'They destroyed the temple as well,' continued Ephiriel. 'Only a small part of the west wall is left. Later this wall will be given the name the Wailing Wall. From this time on the Jews will be scattered over the whole world.'

'It's so silly it almost makes me cry,' whimpered Impuriel. 'We keep on saying "Peace be with you" and "Peace on earth", but humans never seem to learn that they mustn't fight each other. Even though the last thing Jesus said when he was taken prisoner was that those who seize the sword shall perish by the sword.'

Ephiriel agreed. 'All those who celebrate Christmas must remember that. Peace is the message of Christmas.'

'That's what we sing every Christmas night,' continued Impuriel. 'We sing, "Glory to God in the highest and peace on earth!" But it's just as if people don't *want* to listen to that song. Soon I shan't be bothered to sing it any more, so there.'

Joshua struck his shepherd's crook against the top of the Mount of Olives and said, 'To Bethlehem! To Bethlehem!'

They sped down through the city. A few people were moving among the ruins. One woman was looking into the ruined buildings as if she was searching for something she had lost.

The pilgrims ran out through the remains of the western city gate and down the road to Bethlehem. They were only a few kilometres away from the city of David.

All of a sudden they caught sight of a man who was walking beside an ass. When he heard the procession approaching he looked up and waved both arms.

'Fear not! Fear not!' shouted Impuriel from a long way away.

But the man was not in the least afraid.

'Then he is one of us,' said Ephiriel.

The man with the ass came towards them. He offered his hand to Elisabet.

'I am the innkeeper. I am the one who will say that there's no room for Mary and Joseph. But I shall lend them the stable instead.' Whereupon he lifted Elisabet on to the back of the ass. 'You must be tired after your long journey,' he said.

Elisabet shook her head. 'I've run through the whole of Europe, and through the whole of history as well. Then it goes just as quickly as if you're running down a moving staircase.'

The man stared at her without understanding what she said. 'Did you say "moving staircase"?'

Elisabet nodded.

' "Moving staircase"?' said the man again. 'That's a funny expression. "Moving staircase" . . .'

Joshua struck his crook on the ground: 'To Bethlehem! To Bethlehem!'

MAMA PUT DOWN the scrap of paper and looked at the others with a solemn expression on her face. Papa said, ' "Out here in the wilderness Jesus was baptised by John the Baptist".'

'I know that,' said Joachim, exactly like the angel Impuriel in the magic Advent calendar. He went on excitedly, 'John the flower-seller is out in the wilderness too. And, he poured water over himself and over the bookseller. Yes, indeed!'

'That can't be accidental, can it?' said Papa. 'And we never thought about his name!'

'People and flowers both need water,' Joachim went on. 'In the magic Advent calendar it said that the wild flowers are part of the glory of heaven that has strayed down to earth. I expect there was a lot of the glory of heaven in the River Jordan too.'

Papa got to his feet and went into the sitting room to fetch the Bible. When he came back he leafed through the pages, then read aloud:

' "The voice of one crying in the wilderness,
Prepare ye the way of the Lord,
make his paths straight.
Every valley shall be filled,
and every mountain and hill shall be brought low;
and the crooked shall be made straight,
and the rough ways shall be made smooth;
and all flesh shall see the salvation of God." '

'That was poetic,' said Mama.

'In a way this is what the whole of the magic Advent calendar is trying to tell us,' said Papa. 'The pilgrims have been travelling towards Bethlehem, but as well as that they have seen how the stories about Jesus have spread over the whole world.'

'Perhaps so,' said Mama. 'But I shan't be satisfied until we've solved the mystery of who Elisabet the first, and the second, and the third, are.'

They had to hurry to work and to school. This was the day that Joachim's class was going to perform a nativity play for other pupils, and Joachim was going to be one of the shepherds.

On the way home the thought came to him that nearly all the pilgrims who had taken part in the long pilgrimage in the magic Advent calendar had taken part in the school nativity play as well.

As he was letting himself into the house, he noticed a letter stuck in the crack of the door. He drew it out and read the envelope. It said, 'To Joachim'!

He hurried indoors and sat down on the stool in the hall. Then he opened the letter and read what was written on a thin piece of paper:

Dear Joachim, I am inviting myself to a cup of coffee and a Christmas cookie or two on Little Christmas Eve at seven p.m. I hope the whole family will be there. Yours, John.

Joachim waited until they were sitting at the dinner table before telling Mama and Papa about the letter.

'I had a letter from John today,' he began, struggling to keep back a big smile.

'What?' Papa nearly choked. He got up and stretched out

his hand. 'Let's see!' He must have forgotten that it was wrong to read other people's letters.

But Joachim ran into his room to fetch the letter. He gave it to Papa, and Papa read it aloud to Mama.

'Tomorrow at seven o'clock? We must be here, then!' said Mama.

Papa grinned from ear to ear. 'For "a Christmas cookie or two"! We'll put out everything we've got – macaroon cake as well. Because it's Christmas!'

the
TWENTY-
THIRD
OF DECEMBER

... it was as if all of them were rehearsing something

they had to know by heart ...

IT'S CHRISTMAS! THOUGHT Joachim when he woke on Little Christmas Eve. He was itching to open the last door but one in the magic Advent calendar, but he didn't dare touch it until Mama and Papa were up.

Before long both of them were awake. Papa had taken a day off work. 'Because it's Christmas,' he said again.

Joachim opened the last door but one in the Advent calendar. It was a picture of a man walking beside an ass. On the ass sat a woman in red clothes.

A piece of paper had fallen out of the calendar. Papa unfolded it and read what was written on it. Joachim could see his hand was shaking.

MARY AND JOSEPH

A GODLY COMPANY was on its way to Bethlehem. In a way the procession of pilgrims stretched from the long, narrow countries below the cold North Pole at the top of Europe, right down to warm Judea, which is where Europe, Asia and Africa meet. It stretched from the distant future right back to the beginning of our era.

There were seven godly sheep, four shepherds, three Kings of Orient, five angels of the Lord, the Emperor Augustus, the

Governor Quirinius, the innkeeper, and Elisabet, who was allowed to sit on the back of an ass on the last part of the journey to the city of David.

They moved along more and more slowly until they were going at an ordinary walking pace. Ephiriel said that the angel watch had stopped at the year 0. He pointed to a city far away and said that was Bethlehem.

At once the Emperor Augustus halted and put his sceptre into the ground under an olive tree. He stood up straight, opened the book he had been carrying under his arm and said in a commanding voice, 'The time has come!'

They all remained standing on the road, and the Emperor continued: 'I order you all to write your names in the census.'

He held up a piece of charcoal and handed it to each one of the pilgrims in turn. Then they all wrote their names in the big book, even the angels. Only the sheep were excused, probably because they couldn't write and nobody had given them names.

Elisabet was the last to write her name. She read out all the other names before she added her own signature.

1st shepherd: Joshua
2nd shepherd: Jacob
3rd shepherd: Isaac
4th shepherd: Daniel

1st Wise Man: Caspar
2nd Wise Man: Balthazar
3rd Wise Man: Melchior

1st angel: Ephiriel
2nd angel: Impuriel
3rd angel: Seraphiel

4th angel: Cherubiel
5th angel: Evangeliel

Quirinius, Governor of Syria

Augustus, Emperor of the Roman Empire

Innkeeper

Elisabet added her own name in this way:

1st pilgrim: Elisabet

Then she had a good idea. She thought the sheep ought to be included in the census even though they couldn't write and hadn't been given any names. So she wrote:

1st sheep
2nd sheep
3rd sheep
4th sheep
5th sheep
6th sheep
7th sheep

She glanced up at the Emperor Augustus. She was afraid he might be angry because she had messed up his census, but he merely slammed the book shut.

Elisabet had worked out that there were twenty-three pilgrims listed in the census if she included herself and the seven sheep. That was as many as a whole class in school.

After they had registered, the pilgrims became a little more solemn than they had been in Scania and Hamelin, in Venice and Constantinople, in Myra and Damascus.

Ephiriel said, ' "Joseph went up from Galilee, out of the city of Nazareth, into Judea, unto the city of David, which is called Bethlehem (because he was of the house and lineage of David) to be taxed with Mary, his espoused wife, being great with child."'

The procession of pilgrims started moving off slowly, but before long Ephiriel said they had to stop again. He pointed down the road. A young man was walking beside an ass, and on the ass sat a woman in red clothes. In the background Bethlehem was spread out over a terraced landscape, with long slopes almost bare of grass because of all the flocks of sheep.

'There are Mary and Joseph,' said Ephiriel. 'For now the time has come, like a ripening fruit.'

'I must hurry to get there before them,' said the innkeeper, and he started running across the hills. As he ran, he muttered to himself, 'No, I'm sorry, we're full up. But you can stay in the stable...'

A certain nervousness transmitted itself to the other pilgrims. It was as if all of them were rehearsing something they had to know by heart.

Impuriel leapt into the air, beat his wings, and said, ' "Fear not: for, behold, I bring you good tidings of great joy, which shall be to all people. For unto you is born this day in the city of David, a Saviour, which is Christ the Lord. And this shall be a sign unto you; Ye shall find the babe wrapped in swaddling clothes, lying in a manger."'

Ephiriel nodded, and Impuriel exclaimed, 'Wonderful!'

Then the angel Evangeliel blew his trumpet, and all five angels chorused together: ' "Glory to God in the highest and on earth peace, goodwill toward men."'

The sheep had suddenly begun bleating. It was as if they, too, had started practising something they had to learn by heart.

Joshua the shepherd turned to the other shepherds.

'"Let us now go, even unto Bethlehem, and see this thing which is come to pass, which the Lord hath made known unto us."'

Finally the Wise Men spoke.

'"Where is he that is born King of the Jews? For we have seen his star in the east, and are come to worship him."'

They knelt down and held out the caskets with gold, incense and myrrh.

The angel Ephiriel nodded with pleasure.

'I think that'll do.'

Joshua laid down his shepherd's crook carefully on the fleece of one of the sheep and whispered, 'To Be-ethle-ehe-em! To Be-ethle-ehe-m!'

PAPA SAT FOR a long time with the piece of paper in his lap before anyone dared to say anything. He had read that a certain nervousness had spread among the pilgrims as they came closer to the stable in Bethlehem. The same thing happened in Joachim's little room too.

'There can be only one Advent calendar like this in the whole world,' said Papa, 'and we're the only people to have been given it.'

Mama nodded. 'And the real Christmas night happened only once, but that Christmas night resulted in Christmas over the whole world.'

'That's because the glory of heaven spreads so easily,' said Joachim. 'I think it must be infectious.'

There was still a lot to do before Christmas Eve. The family tradition was that Mama and Papa decorated the Christmas tree on the evening of Little Christmas Eve after Joachim had gone to bed, but this year they decided they would all three do it before John came. Then everything would be ready for Christmas.

Afternoon came. Mama set the table and put out all the good things they had to eat, including the big macaroon cake.

The clock was striking seven when the doorbell rang.

'You open it, Joachim,' said Mama. 'You were given the magic Advent calendar, and he invited himself to you for coffee.'

He ran to the door. The old flower-seller was standing on the steps outside, smiling broadly. He held a large bouquet of roses.

'Please come in,' said Joachim.

Then Mama and Papa came and John gave Mama the roses.

'Thank you *very* much,' she said, 'and thank you for the wonderful Advent calendar.'

John put his hand on Joachim's head and replied modestly, 'I think perhaps I ought to thank *you*.'

When they were seated, John took a sip of coffee and then began to tell them about himself.

'I was born in Damascus and grew up in a Christian home. Some people think our family goes back to the first congregation in Syria. One day when I was a boy I found an old jar containing scrolls of manuscript that were almost torn to shreds. My parents had the good sense to take it to the museum. There they discovered that the jar was very old. So were the scrolls.'

'What was written on the scrolls?' asked Papa.

'They were various reports from Roman legionaries. Among other things they reported something that happened in Damascus at the end of the second century after Christ. In the year 175 a curious procession is supposed to have come rushing out through the eastern city gate. A few years later a similar procession came rushing *into* the city through the western gate. It was reported that there were some angels in both processions.'

Mama and Joachim nodded, for they remembered what they had read in the magic Advent calendar.

'There are many legends and myths like that from times gone by,' continued John, 'but I was surprised that the procession should have run *out* of the city *before* it ran *into* the city. If it had, it would have had to run backwards in time, and that's quite impossible, of course.'

'Yes, quite impossible,' agreed Papa. He made a sign that John should continue.

'But my interest in myths and legends had been aroused. I began to read old books, and was particularly interested in stories about people who thought they had seen angels. Finally I had a valuable collection of such stories, from my own part of the world and from many countries in Europe. After some years I went to Rome to take advantage of the treasures in the libraries there.'

'And that's where you met Elisabet?' asked Joachim.

John nodded.

'But wait a bit. I had paid attention to only a few of these angel stories because I thought they had something in common. They were from widely differing places, such as Hanover and Copenhagen, Basle and Venice, the Val d'Aosta in Northern Italy and the Axios Valley in Macedonia. But they were from very different periods too. The earliest story was from Capernaum in Galilee and the latest was from Norway – *that* happened on a country road outside Halden as recently as 1916.'

'The vintage car!' said Joachim.

'Of course there are very few people who believe such stories these days. All the stories I had collected said that the sight of the little girl and the angel had lasted only a second or two. But when I compared the stories from Halden, Hanover and Hamelin with the stories from Aosta, Axios and Capernaum – well, then those stories became quite remarkable.'

The flower-seller sat for a while, lost in his own thoughts.

'Something that is mysterious for one second is often quenched like an empty oil lamp in the next,' he said. 'Yet, if only we turn our heads in another direction, a new light may be lighted there. For we cannot take in what is sacred in the same way as we pick up a stone from the ground and put it in our pockets. Angels float down unseen; they don't fall into the middle of the market square.'

'What happened to the young woman in the photo?' asked Papa.

John sighed. Joachim thought he saw a tear in the corner of his eye; at any rate, he put his hand up there.

'Once,' he said, 'many, many years ago I met a young woman in Rome. It was a meeting which lasted only a few weeks, but I became very fond of her.'

'Tell us!' said Papa. 'Tell us about it!'

'She called herself Tebasile and was very secretive. She said she was probably born in Norway, but that she had grown up among shepherds and sheep farmers in Palestine. The latter was certainly correct, for she spoke fluent Arabic. And the name Tebasile sounded fairly Palestinian – although it could just as easily have been Italian.'

'But it's Elisabet backwards!' exclaimed Joachim.

John nodded. 'Yes, you're a sharp one, you are. People don't usually spell their names backwards.'

'Go on!' begged Papa.

'It might have been true that she was Norwegian as well. Her skin was fair, almost peach-coloured, and her eyes were blue and sparkling. When I asked what took her to Palestine she just sat staring into my eyes. She said, "I was kidnapped." I had to ask who had kidnapped her, and she replied, "An angel who needed me in Bethlehem ... but it's so long ago ... I was only a little girl..."'

Mama gasped. 'What did you say?' asked Papa.

'Other people would probably merely have smiled at such a pack of lies. But I thought of all my angel stories. I replied that I believed what she told me. But the very fact that I took her seriously must have scared her.'

'What happened next?' asked Mama.

'We saw each other only once after that. It was on the Way of Reconciliation in front of St Peter's Square. She said she would be leaving Rome the same afternoon. But she let me take a picture of her. That was in April 1961.'

'How did *you* come to Norway?' asked Papa. 'And why?'

John took the top ring of the macaroon cake and said, 'I came here because I hoped to meet that mysterious woman again, and since then I've stayed here. But I've never met her. I've never managed to find the answer to where she might be. But we'll see ...'

He took a bite of the little macaroon ring.

'It wasn't long before I heard about that disappearance in 1948. That was when I began asking myself whether the poor little girl could have been Tebasile, who had said she was kidnapped by an angel when she was a small child. I didn't know exactly how old she was, but it could fit if she had been born in about 1940.'

John was silent for a while. Then he said, 'I noticed the strange similarity in the names only recently. It's a fact that we often repeat the names of people we think about in our minds. One day we suddenly read it backwards. During the early years in Norway I thought about Tebasile almost continually. Then it struck me like a bolt from the blue. When I read her name backwards, it turned into Elisabet! I became even more convinced that I really had met the missing Elisabet all those years later in Rome. That was when I began to make the magic Advent calendar. I was many months making it, you understand.'

'In any case, it was an incredible coincidence,' commented Papa.

'I had to ask myself whether she really could be the one and the same person,' said John. 'After all, it was curious that the one name turned into the other name backwards. This must have happened just after I met Anna, Elisabet's younger sister. It had struck me that Anna was an amusing name that was exactly the same whichever way you read it, from front to back or back to front. Maybe that was why I suddenly spelt Elisabet backwards. Besides, I thought Elisabet's little sister was very similar to Tebasile.'

'Why did you make the Advent calendar?' asked Mama. 'Why didn't you write it all down in a book?'

John laughed. 'You think anyone would have believed in that book? You think any publisher would have published it?'

Mama shook her head, and John said, 'I made the magic

Advent calendar so that at least one person could carry the story of Elisabet and the long pilgrimage further. In that way I hoped that the old mystery might one day be solved. After all, I don't know how much time I have left. But now I'm no longer the only person who knows this strange story.'

'Then you put a picture of Elisabet in the shop window,' said Mama.

John nodded. 'To see whether anyone here in town would recognise her.'

'Why did you travel to the wilderness?' Joachim wanted to know.

And the old flower-seller explained.

'Every Advent I go out to the country and walk in the woods and hills outside town. To find peace before the Christmas festival, but also to see whether I can find any trace of the lamb, Elisabet and the angel Ephiriel who set off for Bethlehem in 1948. I admit it. Sometimes I walk about saying the two names inside my head: Elisabet ... Tebasile ... Elisabet.'

'Have you never wanted to go back to Damascus?' asked Papa.

John shook his head.

'No, this is my home now. I sell flowers at the market, and in that way I can help to spread a little of the glory of heaven around me. That sort of thing is very easily scattered, you know. And one day Elisabet may come back to town. Because there's something else ...'

It was so quiet in the room that they could almost hear dust flakes falling on to the wooden floor.

John said to Joachim, 'All these years I've tried hard to find her again. But I knew only her first name, or so I believed. To find an Elisabet or a Tebasile only by her

Christian name – whether in Rome or in Palestine – well, that's more difficult than to catch a sparrow in your hand. I've been laughed at in embassies and in census offices in quite a few countries. But Joachim...'

Again it was completely silent in the room.

'Joachim may have helped me to find her again. So I'm the one to thank *you*.'

Joachim looked up at Mama and Papa. He couldn't fathom what John was talking about.

'I think you'll have to explain a bit more,' said Mama.

'It was Joachim who set me to thinking that maybe she had both names, one as her first name and the other as her last name. It's strange how lacking in imagination we can be when we're thinking the same thoughts year after year.'

Joachim's face lit up. 'Elisabet Tebasile!' he said. 'Is *that* what she's called?'

'There's a telephone subscriber in Rome who has that name. But it's not Christmas yet. Tomorrow you must open the last door in the magic Advent calendar.'

John got to his feet and said he had to hurry because there was something he had to do.

'But maybe I can have a look at the Advent calendar for the last time?' he said.

Joachim rushed into his bedroom and took the magic Advent calendar down from its hook. When he was back in the sitting room he handed the calendar to John, who stood examining the picture.

'You must push all the open doors shut,' explained Joachim.

So that's what he did. He said, 'Yes, here they all are. Quirinius and the Emperor Augustus, the angels in the sky and the shepherds in the fields, the Kings of Orient and Mary, Joseph and the Christ-child.'

'But not Elisabet,' said Joachim.

'No, not Elisabet.'

They accompanied John to the door. As he was about to leave, he said, 'So we'll have to see what this Christmas will bring.'

'Indeed, we shall,' said Papa. He was clearly relieved to have finally heard the flower-seller's story.

But John said something more.

'You won't open the last door in the Advent calendar until the bells ring Christmas in tomorrow afternoon, will you?'

Mama looked at him. 'No-o-o, I suppose not.'

'No, we'll have to try to wait that long,' decided Papa.

When John was on the steps outside, he said, 'Maybe I'll knock on your door tomorrow as well.'

Joachim was delighted. He felt something bubbling and fizzing deep down inside him. That was because John had said that maybe he'd look in tomorrow too. For Joachim was not as pleased about everything as Mama and Papa were.

Something was still missing, it seemed to him.

the
TWENTY-
FOURTH
OF DECEMBER

... a spark from the great beacon behind those

weak lanterns in the sky ...

CHRISTMAS EVE BEGAN as usual. There was always some last-minute task that had to be done, and last-minute presents to be wrapped up. Now and again one of them would sneak into Joachim's room and glance expectantly at the magic Advent calendar. They had promised not to open it until the bells rang Christmas in.

Later in the day they began to prepare Christmas dinner. Before long the whole house was smelling of Christmas. At last it was five o'clock. Papa opened a window, and now they could hear the church bells ringing.

Nobody said anything, but they all crept into the bedroom. Joachim climbed on to the bed and opened the last, big door in the calendar. It was the one that covered the manger with the Christ-child. The picture beneath it showed a cave in a mountain.

For the last time they sat on the edge of the bed. Joachim unfolded the thin sheet of paper and read aloud to Mama and Papa.

THE CHRIST-CHILD

IT'S THE MIDDLE of the world between Europe, Asia and Africa. It's in the middle of history at the beginning of our era. Soon it will be the middle of the night as well.

A silent crowd is stealing upwards between the houses in Bethlehem. They are a little flock of seven sheep, four shepherds, five angels of the Lord, three Kings of Orient, one Roman Emperor, the Governor of Syria, and Elisabet from the long, narrow country below the North Pole.

The weak glow of oil lamps is streaming from the windows in a few of the simple houses, but most people in the old town have gone to bed for the night.

One of the Wise Men points up at the sky where the stars are burning in the darkness. They are like sparks from a beacon far away. One star is shining more brightly than all the other stars in the sky. It looks as if it's hanging a little lower in the sky as well.

> 'O little town of Bethlehem,
> How still we see thee lie.
> Above thy deep and dreamless sleep
> The silent stars go by,'

murmurs Elisabet softly, remembering an old carol.

The angel Impuriel turns towards the others, puts a finger to his lips, and whispers, whispers, 'Hush . . . Hush . . .'

The procession of pilgrims gathers in front of one of the inns of the town. In a moment or two the innkeeper appears at the window. When he sees the group outside he nods firmly and points to a cave in the wall of rock.

The angel Ephiriel whispers something; it sounds like the words of a nursery rhyme.

' "And while they were there, the time came for her child to be born, and she gave birth to her son, her first-born. She wrapped him in swaddling clothes, and laid him in a manger, because there was no room for them in the inn." '

They creep across the yard and stop in front of the cave. The smell from it tells them that it is a stable.

Suddenly the silence is broken by the cry of a child.

It is happening now. It is happening in a stable in Bethlehem.

Over the stable a star is twinkling. Inside the stable the new-born child is wrapped in swaddling clothes and laid in a manger.

This is a meeting of heaven and earth. For the child in the manger is also a spark from the great beacon behind those weak lanterns in the sky.

This is the wonder. It is a wonder every time a new child comes into the world. This is how it is when the world is created anew under heaven.

A woman is breathing deeply and weeping. Not out of sadness. Mary is weeping quietly, deeply and happily. But the child's cries drown out Mary. The Christ-child is born. He has been born in a stable in Bethlehem. He has come to our miserable world.

The angel Ephiriel turns solemnly towards the other pilgrims and says, ' "Unto you is born this day in the city of David a Saviour." '

The Emperor Augustus nods.

'And now it's our turn. Everyone is to take up their places, everyone must remember their lines. We have rehearsed this for almost two thousand years.'

Quirinius speaks, at a sign from the Emperor.

'Shepherds! Take your flock out into the fields, and never

forget to be Good Shepherds. Wise Men! Depart to the desert and mount your camels, each one of you. May you never cease to read the stars in the sky. Angels! Fly high above the clouds, all of you. Do not reveal yourselves to people on earth unless it is absolutely necessary, and never forget to say, "Fear not!" For now Jesus is born.'

The next moment all the shepherds and sheep, the angels and the Wise Men, had vanished. Elisabet was left alone with Quirinius and the Emperor Augustus.

'I must hurry home to Damascus,' said Quirinius. 'I have an important role to play there.'

'And I must go back to Rome,' said Augustus. 'That is my role.'

Before they went, Elisabet pointed at the stable and asked, 'Do you think I may go in?'

The Emperor smiled from ear to ear.

'Of course you are to go in. That is *your* role.'

Quirinius nodded energetically.

'You haven't come all this long way just to hang about.'

With those words the two Romans started running back along the way they had come.

Elisabet looked up at the starry sky. She had to tilt her head far back to see the big star which was shining so brightly. Again she heard the cry of a child from inside the cave.

So she went into the stable.

PAPA GOT UP from the bed and punched Joachim on the shoulder.

'Well, we certainly took a remarkable Advent calendar home with us this year,' he said.

He seemed to have finished with it all.

Joachim wasn't as pleased as he was. For what had happened to Elisabet? Mama sat for a while, thinking too. When she got to her feet at last, she said, 'Christmas dinner will be ready soon. Perhaps you could put the presents under the tree while we're waiting. There are a few little surprises this year as well.'

That was exactly what she said. Then the doorbell rang. It was Joachim who opened it again, and again old John was standing outside. Today he was beaming even more than yesterday.

'I've come just to thank you,' he said.

Mama and Papa hurried up and beckoned him in. The macaroon cake was put out on the table again. Only the topmost ring was missing. Papa had put a ball of red marzipan on it instead. Joachim brought out coffee cups and plates.

They sat round the coffee table and John looked at all three of them in turn. He had a mysterious expression on his face.

'When I drew the large picture on the magic Advent calendar,' he said, 'I tried to do it in such a way that there would always be something new to discover. All God's creation was like that, I thought. The more we understand, the more we see in things around us, and the more we see in things around us, the more we understand. So there will always be something new to discover if we only have our eyes and ears open to the remarkable world we live in.'

Papa nodded, and John went on, 'But I didn't know that the calendar was made so that the person who read the scraps of paper would also solve the old mystery of the little girl who disappeared from town almost fifty years ago.'

'Have you found out something more about Elisabet?' asked Joachim.

But John didn't have time to answer, for the next moment the doorbell went again.

Mama looked at Papa, and Papa looked at Mama.

'You'd better open it, Joachim,' said John. 'I expect you're the person who has opened all the doors in the magic Advent calendar. Now you must open this last door as well. But you must open it from the inside.'

As he crossed the floor Joachim noticed that Mama and Papa were holding hands. Surely they weren't afraid that it might be the angel Ephiriel come to visit?

When he opened the front door a woman aged about fifty was standing there. She was wearing a red coat and had fair hair with a little grey in it. The woman gave him a big smile and held out her hand.

'Joachim?' she said.

Joachim felt a bit dizzy but he knew who she was, so he shook her hand.

'Elisabet Hansen,' he said. 'Won't you come in?'

When they came into the sitting room Mama and Papa were still sitting holding hands. Now the old flower-seller gave up keeping a straight face and burst out laughing.

Joachim thought he was a bit like Bishop Nicholas in the magic Advent calendar.

Elisabet was left standing in the middle of the room with her red coat over her arm. Round her neck she was wearing a silver cross set with a red stone.

When John at last managed to stop laughing, he got up from his chair and said, 'Perhaps I should introduce you. This is Elisabet Tebasile Hansen – one and the same person. I came a few minutes ahead of her, but here she is.'

Mama and Papa looked confused, so just in case, Joachim stood in front of them and started to flap his arms. 'Fear not!' he said. 'Fear not! Fear not!'

Only then did they get up from the sofa to shake Elisabet's hand. Mama took her coat and brought another chair, Papa went to fetch another coffee cup from the kitchen.

It appeared that she spoke only English. When they had all sat down again, Papa spoke in Norwegian all the same.

'I think I must ask for an explanation,' he said. 'I think I must almost demand a *proper* explanation.'

'And I'll give it in Norwegian, for the boy's sake,' said John. 'It's to his credit that we are all able to be here today.'

It looked as if the woman with the necklace understood what he was saying, for she looked down at Joachim and smiled.

'Go on!' said Papa.

'When I came to see you yesterday I knew already that Elisabet was on her way to Norway,' began the flower-seller.

'Why didn't you *tell* us?' cried Mama.

John chuckled. 'One doesn't open a Christmas present before Christmas Eve. Besides, I couldn't be quite sure whether she really would come. I couldn't even be quite sure *who* would be coming.'

Papa had begun to shake his head. For a while it looked as if he would never get it back straight again.

'No, I don't understand this,' he said.

So John explained what had happened.

'It began several days ago when I talked to Joachim on the phone. For many years I've tried to trace either a certain Elisabet or a certain Tebasile – for I was convinced that she was one and the same person. But it was Joachim who hinted to me that perhaps Elisabet used Tebasile as her last name. I called Information, was given a telephone number in Rome, and rang her. It didn't take long for her to remember me from those magic days in April 1961.'

Elisabet tried to say something, but John interrupted her with a wave of his hand.

'I told her the story of a mother who had lost her child in 1948. That's how I could tell her who she was. She came to town late yesterday evening. She has not set foot in this place since she disappeared that December day forty-five years ago.'

Papa jumped up from the sofa and went to the phone.

'What is it?' asked Mama.

'I promised to phone Mrs Hansen as soon as I heard anything new.'

John laughed. 'Elisabet stayed with her mother last night. They scarcely closed their eyes, but everything is in good order, I assure you.'

'Well, then I must phone the police,' insisted Papa, 'so that they can close the old case of the girl who disappeared.'

'That's been arranged as well,' replied John. 'You can't have heard the news today. The whole country is delighted about it.'

Papa sank back on the sofa. There was nothing more for

him to do. He could only sit and listen to the rest of what John had to tell.

'May I ask a question?' he said. 'Exactly what *did* happen in December 1948? And don't tell me that Elisabet set off after a lamb and met an angel called Ephiriel.'

He turned towards Elisabet and asked her the same question in English. She put a hand to her mouth to keep back an explosion of laughter, and signed to John that he should answer.

'She always begins to laugh when we talk about that,' explained John. 'We can't agree on it. I'll give you Elisabet's explanation first. She thinks the police in this town did a very bad job. But I think we should begin at the other end.'

'Begin at whatever end you like, as long as you can get the ends to meet,' said Papa.

'Elisabet grew up in a little village near Bethlehem,' said John. 'The people there lived off the poor land they tilled, but even this poor land was taken away from them. When I met Elisabet in Rome in the spring of 1961 she had lived in different refugee camps, first in Jordan, afterwards in Lebanon. She went to Rome in order to explain the refugees' situation. Well, never mind, we can talk about that later. But Elisabet really did go to Bethlehem in December 1948. She came to poor, persecuted people who needed God's help. That's what she meant when she said she had been kidnapped by an angel. She meant she had been kidnapped by someone who wanted to help the people in the villages round Bethlehem. She grew up there as a shepherd girl, so she was able to stroke the soft fleece of the lambs at an early age – just like Elisabet Hansen in the magic Advent calendar.'

'So she suddenly disappeared in Rome,' said Papa. 'Why didn't she want to see you again?'

'I've asked myself that question many times in the years that have passed since then. The answer is that she had to be very careful about who she talked to. That was why she turned her name upside down and took Tebasile as her surname. We mustn't forget that there was a war in the country she came from. Elisabet was afraid of being kidnapped again.'

'Go on!' said Papa.

'When I told her I believed her angel story her suspicions were aroused. She was afraid I might be a dangerous person where her own safety was concerned, and for the Palestinian people.'

'But wasn't Elisabet Norwegian?' Mama wanted to know.

'Yes, she *was* Norwegian,' answered John. 'Elisabet thinks she was kidnapped by some very unhappy people who were willing to do almost anything so that the world should have its eyes opened to the suffering of the Palestinian people.'

'All the same, it was dreadful to kidnap an innocent child,' said Mama.

'Of course you're quite right. Elisabet thinks they must have intended to take her back. Perhaps the people who kidnapped her wanted to try to get her father to write in the papers about all the people who were driven from village to village and finally herded into huge refugee camps outside their own country.'

'So why wasn't she taken back?' interrupted Papa.

'Elisabet says she remembers very little until she was looked after by a big family in the tiny village outside Bethlehem.'

'And what is *your* explanation?' asked Mama.

'You know what that is already,' said John.

Joachim was sitting on the edge of his chair.

'You think she *did* follow the lamb with the bell and met the angel Ephiriel in the woods?' he asked.

John nodded. 'I still do.'

'No!' said Elisabet.

'Yes!' said John.

'No!' said Elisabet, and laughed.

The others began laughing too.

'You mustn't start quarrelling,' said Joachim. 'And you shouldn't start thumbing your noses at each other, either.'

'I believe Elisabet's story,' said Papa.

'And what about you?' asked John, looking at Mama and Joachim.

'I believe twenty-four times more in John's story,' said Joachim.

'Then I'll have to vote twelve times for John's story and twelve for Elisabet's,' decided Mama. 'Because I think a few angels have flown to Bethlehem this Christmas. And back again here, for that matter.'

'But Joachim is right when he says we mustn't start quarrelling even though we believe slightly different things,' said John. 'That's the message of Christmas too. Maybe it's the greatest of all truths that the glory of heaven is easily scattered – at least, if we humans share in dividing it out. When I wrote on those scraps of paper that I folded up so carefully and put inside the magic Advent calendar I had a few clues. I had heard about Elisabet Hansen who disappeared, and I had met Tebasile in Rome. And I had the old angel stories to rely on as well. The rest of it I had to imagine myself.'

Silence fell in the sitting room.

'You managed it very well,' said Mama.

John smiled shyly. 'The imagination, also, is a tiny piece

of the glory of heaven that has strayed down to earth. It, too, can be scattered very easily.'

'It's all amazing,' said Mama. 'We open the last door in an old Advent calendar and hear about Elisabet who goes into a stable in Bethlehem to welcome the Christ-child into the world. Immediately afterwards the same Elisabet rings the doorbell in our own house. So it almost seems as if this house is the same as the stable where Jesus was born.'

She stood up and put her arms round Elisabet. 'Welcome back to Norway, my child,' she said.

That was a funny thing to say, since Elisabet was almost twenty years older than Mama.

'Thank you very much,' said Elisabet, and she said those words in Norwegian.

A little later the phone rang. Papa took it, and Joachim knew at once who he was talking to, because he heard Papa say, 'We're all overwhelmed ... the Christmas present of the year, Mrs Hansen ... Yes, *now* I believe in angels as well ... Here she is ... and a Happy Christmas, a very Happy Christmas to all your family ...'

Papa made a sign to Elisabet and gave her the receiver. She spoke English, so Joachim couldn't understand what she was saying, but he thought it must be strange to talk to your own mother in a foreign language.

Before long Elisabet and John had to leave. But they would all meet again after Christmas because Mama and Papa and Joachim had been invited to a big Christmas party at home with Elisabet's family.

The guests were escorted to the front door. Outside it was snowing heavily.

Papa asked whether Elisabet could remember any Norwegian from when she was small.

She stood under the outside light while the snow poured down on to her red coat. Suddenly she bent down and stretched out her hand as if she was trying to catch the dancing snowflakes.

'Lambkin, lambkin, lambkin!' she said.

She put her hand up to her mouth in alarm. The next moment she started running. A few seconds later she and the old flower-seller were gone.

Late that evening, when Joachim was going to bed, he stood for a long time in front of his window, staring out into the Christmas night. There had been a huge fall of new snow, but now it was clear enough to see the stars.

Suddenly he caught sight of some figures running past down on the road. It was not easy to keep his eyes on them, for he could see them only in the light of the street lamps, and the sight lasted for only a second or two.

Joachim thought he had recognised the angel Ephiriel and all the others who had accompanied Elisabet to Bethlehem.

That night they had escorted her back.